THE WHEEL TRUTH
THE DAHLIA WILDES MAGICAL MYSTERIES
BOOK V

NOVA NELSON

FFS Media

For the community of readers who choose to spend their time in Eastwind. You are the reason I choose to spend my time there as well. The realm would be nothing without each of you.

Contents

Chapter One

"Would it kill you to tell the truth?" asked Nora Ashcroft, glaring at her shaggy hellhound familiar, Grim, where he lay behind the counter of Medium Rare.

"*I didn't eat it,*" he replied.

It was obvious, even without my gift of Empathy, to tell that Nora was more stressed than usual. My unofficial mentor was trying to juggle too many things. Today, it was a busy Friday morning at the diner she owned with her husband Tanner—who was too busy in his own line of work to help out anymore—while wrapping up loose ends before heading out of town for the weekend. And, oh yeah, *someone* had scarfed scrambled eggs and bacon off a breakfast platter when she'd set it down for one second to grab the coffee pot.

Considering his record, I didn't think it was too big of an assumption to pin it on Grim.

"It's not like I can discipline you anyway," she said,

shaking her head at the hellhound. She looked up at me where I sat on one of the high stools at the countertop. "Did you see him do it, Dahlia?"

I shook my head. I'd been too busy looking behind me, wondering when my boyfriend would arrive to play watchdog to a plate of food that wasn't mine.

"Don't you think I'd tell you if it was me?" Grim replied. Nora *used* to be the only one who could hear Grim's telepathic communication, the kind each witch shared with their familiar, but one of the gifts I'd discovered—for better or worse—was that I could eavesdrop on this particular kind of conversation.

I tried not to, but it wasn't always in my power to ignore it.

Nora rolled her eyes. "I suppose you're usually pretty shameless about it, yeah." Her eyes flickered to the white hellhound asleep on the linoleum floor next to Grim, but she didn't accuse my familiar, Atlas, of anything.

I was grateful of that. While Atlas was large and intimidating to anyone who didn't know him personally, he was skittish. He'd made leaps and bounds in his courage since leaving the Deadwoods, where he'd been bullied pretty relentlessly by the other hellhounds for his white coat, so I decided not to interrogate him about the plate of food and risk setting him back.

Nora jotted down the order for the missing food, sent it to the kitchen, then returned to the counter. "When do you and Tanner leave?" I asked.

She exhaled sharply. "Our train leaves in an hour and a half."

"The train to Avalon?" I asked.

She nodded. "Wisconsin is attached to Avalon, so we have to pass through."

The diner was packed. It was a Friday morning, and everyone seemed to be slacking off work at the end of the week. Plus, the tourists usually started flooding the town on Fridays now. It had become a real problem in some ways, but many Eastwinders appreciated the extra customers.

Nora wasn't one of those people. Medium Rare had always had enough customers to keep its doors open. Now she struggled to keep enough employees on staff to handle the constant crowds. She'd started putting little "reserved" signs on some of the tables to make sure the local regulars had a place to sit whenever they came in. They knew to ignore the signs, but the tourists didn't.

"Have you ever been to Wisconsin before?" I asked.

"Not this one," she said.

I knew what she meant. Wisconsin was a state in the realm where both she and I had come from before dying and entering Eastwind. But here, it was its own realm, a densely forested vacation spot. I'd only ever heard about werebears and werewolves visiting it before, though.

"I've never even been to Avalon before," she said. "I'm over the sprawling city lifestyle, though, so I'm okay with just passing through— Jaymes!" The young, dark-haired server looked up from where he was chatting with a table of werewolves, and she pointed him toward a group of tourists who were trying to ignore the "reserved" sign on a table. He quickly nodded and hurried over to run them off. If my memory served, that table was usually reserved for the Tomlinsons.

Nora apologized for the lapse in her attention, and I assured her it was fine.

"You're going with Jane and Ansel, right?" I asked.

Nora nodded, and for the first time, she cracked a small smile, like the idea of a weekend getaway wasn't *entirely* a chore. "It'll be nice to have them with us."

I sensed a small shiver of fear emanating from her, and I thought I knew what that was about. "You'll be safe there," I said. "Jane wouldn't let anything happen to you."

Nora narrowed her eyes at me. She was never thrilled when I read the emotions she was trying to hide —most people weren't—but it wasn't like I could help it when someone radiated them strongly. I wasn't as in control of my Fifth Wind powers yet as I'd have liked to be. Still needed much more training. I'd been practicing, but... I'd also been busy working at the pottery studio.

"I know I'll be safe," she said. "I'm less worried about that. It's more that I'm not sure I'll be welcome there. You know I don't have a problem with weres of any kind —I run a business in the Outskirts, for fang's sake. But, well, it's a were-run lodge we're staying at. I don't want to cramp anyone's style or show up somewhere I'm not welcome. Not everyone is as comfortable with Fifth

Winds or even witches in general as Eastwinders. There's a lack of exposure to it in most realms."

"I don't think you'll be cramping anyone's style," I said. "Jane goes there a lot, doesn't she? She wouldn't take you somewhere you're not welcome."

"Hm." Nora considered it as she wiped a small bead of sweat from her forehead with the back of her wrist. She scanned the diner and, apparently satisfied that nothing needed immediate action, returned her attention to me. "You gonna be okay while I'm gone?"

I tried my best to assure her with a smile. "Of course. I've been on my own for most of my life. I can take care of myself. I always have."

"To be fair," she replied, "you did die once."

I laughed. "So did you!"

Nora shrugged. "Nobody's perfect."

"Look," I said, "you deserve a vacation more than anyone I know. Jaymes and Bryant will keep this place from burning down"—she knocked superstitiously four times on the countertop—"and I'm sure Eastwind can go a weekend without needing any Fifth Wind services." I paused, then *I* knocked four times on the countertop, just in case.

"If it does come to that," she said, "which I obviously hope it doesn't, Ted has already agreed to help you out as much as possible."

She nodded over my shoulder, and I turned to find the grim reaper sitting in his usual spot in the corner booth. He looked up from his crossword and waved.

Nora and I waved back. Ted was one of the only people in Eastwind who could see and speak to spirits of the dead like Nora and I could, so he wouldn't be a bad person to have around on an investigation.

But it won't come to that! This town goes weekends without a murder all the time. This will be no different.

"Famous last words," said Atlas, overhearing my thoughts.

The bell over the diner door rang, and in walked Dante Fontaine. He paused to look around for me. I still felt butterflies in my stomach every time I saw my boyfriend, even though we'd been together for months now.

Our relationship had experienced a few bumps in the road, sure, but mostly we were great. And every time something came up, we found a way of talking through it that made me feel even closer to him, more connected. I'd never felt this way about anyone before. It was wonderful.

And strangely unsettling as well. I sometimes felt overwhelmed by that feeling in a way that made my brain fuzzy. After a lifetime of being able to creep around like a mouse, totally invisible to most people, being so seen by him felt... disconcerting, to say the least.

Nora leaned over the counter, muttering, "Siren's song, you got a handsome one. If I were unmarried and ten years younger..."

I swatted her playfully on the arm, and she laughed.

"I'll grab him some coffee."

Chapter Two

Atlas belched audibly and somewhat suspiciously as we left the diner and passed through the run-down buildings of the Outskirts, making for the center of town.

Dante was nervous. He normally projected a together exterior—calm, steady, unflappable, often unreadable. Sure, he occasionally lost his temper and fought someone, but in his defense, it was always, to my knowledge, someone who probably needed to be put in their place.

Ninety-nine percent of the time, he was an anchoring presence for most people.

Unfortunately, I could tell when something was off where others couldn't. There were only three Fifth Wind witches in town, and very little information about our powers was available at the Eastwind Library, so no one knew much about our kind. Besides Nora and me, there was Ruby True, who had retired years before, no longer wanting to participate in the murder investigations that a psychic witch was especially suited for. Ruby had passed the baton to Nora, who was now passing it along to me more and more frequently.

What we were all learning, though, was just how much variety there could be in our individual powers. The "fifth wind" was that of the spirit, and the spirit involved itself in all sorts of things.

We could each see ghosts, yes, but Ruby had other strange abilities, some of which looked more like the other four types of witches, and Nora had her own bag of tricks, which included something called Quenching where she sucked the light out of the space, a thing that I'd never seen her do but hoped I'd one day unlock for myself.

My unique gifts, as far as I could tell, had to do with the spiritual realm of… emotions. Ugh. Not my first pick. In general, I preferred to tune out any strong emotions. They were incredibly disruptive to a peaceful and easy life. Emotions often asked one to take action that stirred up more trouble than I preferred. If I wasn't careful, they even led to conflict. Hard pass on that!

Prior to my dying and coming to Eastwind, if you'd asked me what my magical power would be, I'd have guessed invisibility. I was great at going unnoticed. It's a talent you pick up when you learn that people can't clash with what they don't see or sense. I was a fantastic house cleaner as a result of my ability to creep around like a mouse. The way I could make a house—poof!—clean without anyone noticing I was there was its own kind of magic in a mostly non-magical realm.

But now that I was in Eastwind, and had been for roughly half a year, I'd given up on the luxury of invisibility. As a Fifth Wind witch who could speak with the dead and communicate with all familiars (I kept that bit as much of a secret as I could, because I knew it would anger a lot of witches), there was no getting around the fact that I was here, I was special, and I wasn't going anywhere anytime soon.

It was a sunny, late-spring day, the kind where it's hard for any negative thoughts to dig their claws in. And yet Dante was definitely nervous. I didn't have to ask why. I knew the cause.

"You only need one of the pieces to come out of the kiln like you'd hoped, right?" I asked.

We strolled through Fulcrum Park on the way to Time to Kiln, where the final day of the big pottery competition would begin shortly, starting with the unloading of the kiln.

I was anxious for Dante, too. I'd only thrown on the pottery wheel at the studio for a short time, but I'd learned how unpredictable results could be coming out of the final firing. There were so many opportunities for a project to be ruined at various points throughout the process. That was why each contestant had been allowed to create five pieces on the first day of the competition. Pieces could crack as they dried, you could trim through the bottom, it could split in the bisque firing, or the glaze could drip and stick the whole thing to the shelf in this final phase. Oh, and there were also all kinds of opportunities for people to drop things. You might be surprised how much that was the issue. Holding on to things suddenly became much trickier, apparently, when the stakes were high.

"I had three pieces left going into the glazing," he said, his brows pinched together. "I took a risk by over-lapping two glazes on the teapot. One of them can be runny. On the bird feeder, I'm worried I didn't wax enough of the bottom..."

As he ran through his list of possible disasters, I struggled to follow along. I cared deeply about Dante and wanted him to have all the success he dreamed of, but I usually found my brain tuning out when people went through worst-case scenarios (my own brain could come up with enough on its own, thank you). And besides, it was a such a beautiful day. The trees around Fulcrum Fountain bloomed with little pink blossoms that covered their branches and drifted to the emerald grass below them like snowflakes when the wind blew.

As we turned off onto one of the main side streets stretching out like spokes from Fulcrum Park, the large, temporary tent outside of Time to Kiln came into view, peeking up from the center of a large crowd.

The studio and shop weren't nearly big enough to house all the locals and tourists who were gathering to see the show.

This was the main event in Eastwind this week, and

on top of that, Raven and Jude, the owners of Time to Kiln, had somehow managed to secure one of the most famous potters in Eastwind and the connecting realms as a judge.

Orville Ironhelm, a short goblin whose skin was a greener shade than most of the goblins I'd seen around Eastwind, was apparently a pottery legend, even in Avalon. To be renowned in such a big and bustling realm meant you really had some talent.

If I hadn't already understood how big of a deal securing this particular judge was, the way Dante had gaped at him in complete and utter awe throughout every day of this competition would've told me all I needed to know.

Dante wasn't easily impressed, but his admiration for Orville broke through his steady expression.

The final judging didn't start until noon, about a half-hour away, but the crowd was already waiting. The judges' table was unoccupied, but the biggest pottery enthusiasts had claimed their spots nearby.

I searched the crowd for familiar faces and easily found a few. Grace Merryweather and her husband Landon Hawker were on the other side of the crowd. Their five-year-old son Monte was seated on Landon's shoulders, getting a better view than most. I didn't love being near crowds, and enjoyed being in the middle of them even less, due to the overwhelming emotions that usually accompanied it, so I settled for waving at my friends. Grace waved back and showed no signs of trying to weave her way over to me, either.

I'd been practicing some of my shields against emotions with Nora's help, but I was still a long way from wanting to dive into the center of a crowd if I had other options.

Jude Fangly, one of the owners of Time to Kiln, and consequently my boss as well, appeared next to us as we reached the periphery of the gathered onlookers. The quiet werewolf was more involved in the artistic side of running the studio than the business side, and despite the prestigious event where the host might want to dress to impress, he wore navy-blue cotton pants and a loose-fitting tan shirt, both with splotches of dried clay and glaze stains across them. He rested a hand gently on Dante's shoulder to get his attention. "We're about to unload the kiln. I'm gathering all the contestants around to watch it together." Jude offered me a warm smile. "As a Time to Kiln employee, you're welcome to join us, Dahlia."

"I'd love to."

I was less interested in the process of unloading and more interested in providing Dante moral support on the off chance that none of his pieces came out the way he'd hoped. Jude was an excellent kiln operator, but sometimes strange things happened outside of his control. Even a sudden weather shift could affect what happened inside the kiln.

When we arrived at the kilns behind the studio,

Atlas and I set up at the back of the group. I knew a few of those who'd chosen to participate in the competition, like Sasha Cosmo, who held the same position I did at the studio, manning the shop and managing some of the basic inventory. The elf was a much more experienced and skilled potter than I was, hence why she'd entered this competition and I hadn't even bothered.

I was still very much a novice and preferred to be that way without any judgment. I'd recently managed to make a mug I very much liked, even though the handle had dried slightly wonky, and the whole thing was much smaller than I'd planned by the time it made it through the firing process. Even still, I was happy with my mug, and I wasn't interested in anyone else's opinion on it.

Those competing in this battle, though, were so much farther along. Sasha, for instance, specialized in ethereal-looking decorations on slender clay bodies. She had a signature style, in other words, which was something I could only dream of having someday. If I had a signature style at the moment, it was *That sort of looks like what I meant it to be.*

I recognized a few of the other contestants who were longtime students or co-op members of the studio and came in at least once a week to throw or hand-build. I didn't know all of their names, since most of them kept to themselves and didn't bother chatting me up, but I did smile at Margot Penumbra when she caught my eye in the crowd around the kiln. She smiled back. She was a friendly West Wind witch in her mid-forties with dark, gray-streaked hair that she always kept in a loose bun at the top of her head. While I didn't know much about her personal life, she always sang, "Hello, Dahlia!" every time she came into the studio.

As Jude asked everyone to take a step back so he could open the kiln door, Margot snaked through the group toward me. "Hello, Dahlia!" she said. "Here cheering on your lucky guy?"

"I'm cheering on everyone," I replied. "I hope everything comes out of the kiln in fantastic shape."

"Me too. You hate to see something someone's spent so much time on come out cracked or stuck to the kiln. Even if I'm competing with them, I'd rather us all have something we're proud of to finish things off." She leaned closer to keep from being overheard. "Between us, I'm less worried about winning the whole thing and more nervous about what Orville Ironhelm will say about my work. Is that silly?"

"I don't think it's silly at all," I said honestly. "I bet most people here feel the same. He's a big deal in the pottery world."

She nodded. "He doesn't seem particularly happy to be back in Eastwind, have you noticed?"

I looked at her. "*Back* in Eastwind? What do you mean?"

"His family is from here originally. You didn't know that? No, of course you wouldn't. I forget you're new here because you fit in so seamlessly with the community. That's a compliment, of course." She paused. "He was the last Ironhelm here, I believe. I'm honestly shocked they convinced him to come back, even just for a week."

The name Ironhelm wasn't completely foreign to me, but the context in which I'd heard it mentioned before was so vastly different from pottery that my brain hadn't put the two pieces together. "Ironhelm Penitentiary?" I said. "Is that connected to his family?"

Margot nodded. "Not a legacy I'd be particularly proud of, but it's certainly a legacy. I think they used to own other things around Eastwind, but then something must've happened, because I don't remember there being a single Ironhelm in Eastwind in all my time."

"They must've moved to Avalon," I suggested.

"Probably that. And now he's back here judging this contest. Oh, my stomach is absolutely in knots thinking about it! No idea how Jude and Raven managed to book him. Look! Jude's pulling out the first pieces!"

I hung back with Atlas as Margot squeezed in closer to the kiln.

The first piece was easily identifiable as a bird feeder when Jude held it up. "Whose is this?"

Dante raised his hand. "Mine."

The pieces had already cooled, and where some might've worn mitts as a precaution, Jude didn't bother. His hands were rough from years of his work. As he slowly moved the bird feeder toward the table by his side, the bottom piece suddenly dropped off it, crashing to the ground and shattering.

There was a sharp intake of air from the onlookers, myself included, followed by a wave of mixed emotions. Mostly it was empathetic pain, but there was certainly a little bit of satisfaction coming from the more competitive contestants.

"Fang's sake," muttered Dante, staring down at the shattered piece of his feeder. He let out a long sigh, and I squeezed between two other contestants to place a gentle hand on his arm.

"I'm sorry," I whispered.

He rolled his shoulders back. "It's fine. I knew the bottom piece was heavy and that I might not have joined it well enough. I still have two more pieces in the kiln."

I took a step back and crossed my fingers.

The next one Jude lifted into the air was an elegant vase with a pearlescent white glaze. "Whose is this?"

Margot raised her hand. "Mine."

"Could do with a little more precision on the waxing," said Jude. He blinked. Margot appeared stunned. Then she broke out into a wide grin.

Jude set the vase on the table. "I'm sorry, I don't know why I said that."

Margot was still grinning. "You're not wrong. I got a little sloppy with the wax."

He stared down at the vase. "No, but it's quite beautiful, overall. I've never seen that glaze before."

"It's a secret recipe," she said. "Made it myself."

"Stunning, stunning." He returned to the kiln to remove the next entry.

By the time the kiln was fully unloaded, every single contestant had at least one piece that made it through and could be presented to the judges. I was grateful for that.

Dante was happy with the way the glaze had turned out on his teapot. It hadn't run and stuck to the kiln shelf like he'd feared. Instead, it reminded me of a brilliant sunset, transitioning from a midnight blue at the top to a fiery orange toward the bottom. I was surprised myself that the blue hadn't completely overwhelmed the brilliance of the orange, but mostly I was proud of him as we returned to the tent to wait by the judges' table for the final scoring to begin.

Since I wasn't a contestant myself, I couldn't stand right next to Dante, where he gathered with the other competitors. Instead, I found a spot nearby, toward the front of the crowd so I wasn't completely surrounded in a sea of feelings and could keep an eye on both my boyfriend and the judges, when they finally arrived and took their seats.

Sudden applause from the crowd caused Atlas to press up against my side nervously. The judges had entered the tent.

There were three of them total. The first one was obviously Orville Ironhelm, which nobody could stop chattering about. The goblin looked like he'd rather be anywhere else as a young witch, presumably his assistant, led him over to his spot at the table. I wasn't always good at spotting what kind of creature someone was—it was often hard to tell a witch from a were until they whipped out a wand or transformed into an animal—but the assistant wore her wand in a leather holster at her hip. I assumed the bright pastel clothes she wore were fashionable in Avalon, but they felt a bit out of place among the richer colors usually worn in Eastwind. She wore thick glasses that must've been magically secured, as they didn't seem to slip an inch down her nose as she was forced to lean over to speak quietly with Orville as he settled in at the table. Orville forced what could almost count as a smile and waved begrudgingly at the crowd, as if he knew it was their pleasure for him to be here. The witch assisting him waved her wand and a small teacup appeared on the table in front of him, steam coming off the top of it. He didn't seem to notice, let alone care.

There were a handful of goblins in Eastwind. They didn't tend to be particularly social, so I mostly heard about them from Landon Hawker, who worked with them in the Parchment Catacombs, where Eastwind kept its records. I'd seen one or two at the Eastwind Emporium as they gathered their groceries, and they'd looked about as thrilled as Orville seemed to be. They tended to shuffle around and keep to themselves, and I could appreciate that about them.

Raven Goode was another one of the judges, which made sense considering she was likely the most expert potter, aside from perhaps Jude, in all of Eastwind. She also cared about the appearance of impartiality and displayed that in the way she conducted herself leading up to the competition and throughout it. So, while some of the contestants were her students, it was clear that her personal feelings about them would have little impact on her scoring of their pieces (as much as such a thing were possible).

The last judge of the group had me stumped. I'd even asked Dante why this particular person had been selected, when I'd never seen him making any pottery whatsoever. Dante had merely shrugged and said, "Vampires live a long time. Maybe he used to be a potter." When pushed, he finally admitted, somewhat cynically, "He owns half the town and is the treasurer of the High Council. He gets what he wants."

But why would Count Sebastian Malavic, Eastwind's only vampire and infamous philanthropist, want to judge a pottery competition? It was strange.

I'd only had a few encounters with Malavic, as most people called him when they spoke his name like a curse. I hadn't found any of my interactions with him particularly offensive.

He struck me as selfish, sure. Looking out for himself in whatever way he could. But I also got a sense—and I wasn't sure if this was my Empathy or something else—that there was much more to him, that he had a soft side. Perhaps he hadn't accessed it in a century or so, but I could sense it was there. Admittedly, I'd been accused of seeing the good in people where it wasn't, so perhaps this was a case of that. With the way Nora snarled every time someone mentioned him, you'd think he'd murdered her best friend.

Yet he couldn't be *all* bad, right? Eastwind had allowed him to stick around and be treasurer for the High Council for years and years. Vampires could be fierce, I'd heard, but surely if *everyone* showed up at his castle on the peninsula in the lake, they could run him out of town. To my knowledge, that had never happened. He was still here, still respected by some, and now he was the judge of the big pottery contest along with Raven and Orville.

Even if he knew little about the art and craft of pottery, I could see a benefit to having a layperson's opinion on the final entries.

As the judges were introduced by the emcee, the charismatic genie Liberty Freeman (no surprise there), I paid attention to the varying applause. Raven was the first judge introduced, and she received a warm welcome, especially from locals, as the organizer and owner of the studio. She was also simply a beloved member of the community and would repair broken family heirlooms for free whenever she had the time. I was coming to understand that while South Wind witches like her, those with the power of pyromancy, had a reputation around town as wild and lawless, they were also some of the warmest and fiercest defenders of the community. Ezra Ares, another South Wind who ran Ezra's Magical Outfitters, fit the bill as well. Did he like to turn a profit? Sure. Did he sometimes operate outside of the trade laws of Eastwind? Well, yes. But when I was in danger and couldn't afford the necessary materials to stay safe, he was more than generous in his help to me.

When Count Sebastian Malavic was introduced as the next judge, the applause was, let's say, less enthusiastic. I could feel a mix of confusion and obligation in the crowd as they clapped politely, but no one seemed to be particularly excited about the pick.

That wasn't the case when Orville Ironhelm was introduced, though. The crowd cheered and whooped for quite a while, enough that the goblin actually cracked a smile and waved modestly at the audience.

I wondered briefly how old Orville was. It was strange being in a place where different types of beings had such vastly different lifespans and aged at such peculiar rates. Most elves, for instance, appeared to be in their twenties or thirties by human standards, even if they were a hundred years old. Perhaps Orville looked to be in his seventies by human standards, but was only in his twenties!

That's what happens when you measure everything by your own standards, Dahlia. They probably feel the same frustration trying to gauge the age of a witch!

The first few contestants presented their final pieces to the judges, and it was not long before what type of judge each one was became apparent. We wouldn't know the scores until later, but it was clear that Raven had an eye for the artistic elements, what made the piece unique and stand out. Malavic seemed to come at it from more of a monetary perspective, saying things like, "This could fetch a few gold pieces at a gallery in Avalon," or "You'd be lucky for someone to take this off your hands for free."

Orville, meanwhile, mostly pulled faces as each piece was passed down the line and made it to his hands for inspection. He didn't say much about the first two, forcing Liberty Freeman, ever the showman, to prompt him with leading questions, like, "What do you think about the balance of the piece?" and "Do those imperfections in the clay add to the overall appeal, you think?"

Each time, Orville would grunt, shrug, or mutter something like, "One could say so."

I glanced over at Dante. He had been looking forward to constructive feedback from the expert potter, and it seemed like he might not get it. I was pre-disappointed for him.

"Dante Fontaine," Liberty said, "would you please bring your piece to the judges' table?"

I crossed my fingers for him, though I was pretty sure that didn't do anything magical in Eastwind. If I'd had magic that could help him in that moment, at least to feel calmer, I would've cast it in an instant. As usual, he appeared confident and together, but I knew him better than to think he wasn't all knots on the inside. Or maybe that was just me.

Did I mention that I hate competitions?

Raven offered Dante a warm smile as she accepted his teapot and held it up to catch the light. "Beautiful glazing work. I'm impressed you managed to layer these two without too much running." She turned it around in her hand and pulled off the lid to inspect the inside. "Nice, clean lines for the waxing." She weighed it in her palm. "Hefty. Unlikely to be knocked over. Not the usual delicacy one might expect from a teapot, but not everyone has a purpose for that. Excellent work, Dante."

He nodded appreciatively, and she passed the teapot on to Malavic.

As soon as he picked it up, his brows rose. "I personally like the weight of it. Unexpected. Visually, it's delicate, but it feels sturdy. That element of surprise would certainly prove valuable to the right buyer. I could see an ogre shelling out for something like this. Unsurprising that it came from the mind of a werebear. There's big market for sturdier ceramics among the weres. You couldn't fetch a single copper for this from an elf, sure, but value is in the eye of the beholder. If you need to find a buyer, let me know. I have a few in mind."

Dante thanked the vampire for the compliment, even if it was somewhat backhanded, and turned his attention to Orville Ironhelm.

The goblin rotated the teapot on the table a few times, frowning. "Asymmetrical."

Dante remained planted and stock-still.

When Orville lifted the piece, he shook his head disapprovingly. "The colors don't work. Blue should be on the bottom, not the top." He set down the piece and leaned back in his seat, signaling he was done.

My first impulse was to run to Dante and give him a hug. But when it was obvious that he wouldn't appreciate the show, my second impulse was to strangle Orville with my bare hands for failing to give a single compliment to what was an excellent piece of craftsmanship. There was a certain lack of responsibility the goblin was taking for his celebrity. Didn't he know how much a single compliment from someone of his status could encourage a budding potter to keep working on his craft, keep improving and moving the entire occupation forward?

I would never understand how people in power could either fail to recognize or fail to care how much their words impacted others. They had the power to lift others up and the power to tear them down, and far too many chose the latter.

Shame on Orville, I thought.

Atlas overheard it. *"You don't get to be in the position he's in by being nice to people."*

"That's a cynical thought, Atlas."

"Doesn't make it untrue."

"Look at Liberty," I replied. *"He's possibly the most powerful person in the realm and he's nice."*

"Did you already forget that he released a duplicate of you that almost destroyed your relationship with Dante?"

Ah. Right. That.

"You forgive too easily," said Atlas.

"I'd rather forgive too easily than hold a bunch of grudges."

"Grudges save lives."

With that little PSA from my familiar, I returned my attention to the judging. Dante had rejoined the group of contestants, putting on a brave and confident face, shrugging good-naturedly at one of his friends in the crowd, like, *What are ya gonna do?*

Margot Penumbra was the next one up. As Liberty introduced her, I noticed that she grabbed her vase with a thick cloth to carry it over to the judges' table. She set it in front of Raven, explaining, "This vase is inspired by the body shape of an egret with its wings extended toward the sky. I used a proprietary glaze that's infused with clarity. I hope you like it." She clasped her hands behind her back, waiting for Raven to inspect the work.

"Ah," said the South Wind witch. "Clarity. How wonderful. A bold move to hand it over to the judges. What if the clarity we get isn't favorable to your score?"

Margot grinned playfully. "Then at least I'll have clarity on where you stand."

The audience chuckled at that, and Raven reached forward and grabbed the vase.

As she held it up, she sighed. "It's not the worst thing I've seen, but the caliber of work here isn't nearly high enough to justify the money I've staked on this event. Not with what I had to pay Orville to be here." She blinked, as if someone else had just spoken through her, and quickly set the vase on the table and yanked her hands away from it. "Oh my." She tore her eyes from the piece and forced a sheepish grin at Margot and then the crowd. "Kidding, of course. It's got a wonderfully elegant shape to it. I can certainly see the tribute to an egret." She cleared her throat and turned toward Malavic, nodding at the vase without touching it. "You're up, Count."

Malavic was about the only person at the table who seemed amused by Raven's outburst of... *was* it clarity? It seemed like something else to me. Brutal honesty, perhaps.

"Glad to see you've had a moment of clarity on your investments," he said. Without hesitating, he reached over and grabbed the vase. "I could sell this at auction, sure." Then he set it down in front of him and folded his pale hands on the table. "I, too, have been artistically underwhelmed by every contestant so far, but these sorts of pieces are fine commercially. In my experience, most buyers don't have a single ounce of artistic sense in them and could be sold a lump of yeti dung if you called it rare and exotic. The glaze on this is fine, but I suspect whoever was in charge of firing these pieces didn't know what they were doing."

I felt a bold defensiveness of Jude rise up in me, but I choked it down.

Malavic went on. "Maggie, my dragon, could sneeze and pull off a more consistent firing than has been done here. But considering all that, sure, this piece is fine. Nearly impressive. I could get at least a couple of silver coins for it if I found a wealthy enough buyer with no sense of what anything should cost."

Malavic passed the vase along to the final judge, Orville Ironhelm. "I can't wait to hear *your* take," he said with a sneer.

Orville, who had been watching the other two judges with great interest, hesitated to touch the vase. I couldn't blame him. The clarity spell Margot had used in her glaze seemed to pack quite the punch.

Glazing was always delicate business. Dipping the piece a half-second too long could cause it to go on too thick, changing the color, the sheen, and, when applicable, the potency of the spell involved.

Was that what had happened here? Something was certainly off. I'd never heard Raven speak so openly about the finances of the studio, and in such a public setting, no less. When I tuned into her, as Orville was still staring cautiously at the vase without touching it, I sensed a cloud of shame and regret around her. Poor Raven. She was my boss and had been so kind to me. I wanted to give her a hug, but I didn't think she would appreciate it; she was doing her best not to show any of the emotions my Empathy was picking up.

"What?" said Malavic, smirking smugly at Orville. "Scared to experience a little clarity? Afraid of what you might see... or say?"

Orville's expression hardened into hateful determination. Sebastian Malavic had a knack for pressing the right button in people.

The goblin reached forward, grabbed Margot's vase, and pulled it toward him to inspect. "Hm!" His heavy brows shot up. "Actually, lovely." He weighed it in his hands, moved it from side to side to feel the balance, held it up to the light to inspect the glazing. "Slight issue with the wax on the bottom, but nothing the average person would notice or even care about. Easily the best piece I've seen in this entire competition. When I saw you during the throwing stage, Miss Penumbra, I assumed you had no talent or vision in you at all." Margot didn't appear to know how to react to that as she nodded noncommittally, but I could tell she was bracing herself. "I was wrong about that. This is an easy winner, from what I've seen thus far. Had I not already accepted a hefty payment from Mr. Shoehorn to cast my vote for him as the winner"—the crowd gasped, myself included, but Orville didn't seem to notice what he'd just admitted to—"I would stand firmly behind this piece. The movement you've managed to evoke with the curves, the structural balance, the visually intriguing fade from peach to rose with these shimmering crystals that catch the light just right. One of the best pieces I've seen from an amateur in all my years. Perhaps it's a stroke of luck that it all came together like this more than it is a measure of your talent, but even still. It only takes one win for someone to break out. That's why I charge so much for someone to buy my vote. Perhaps a part of me wishes that weren't the way things worked in the realms, but it is. Money is power. Money buys dreams, it buys success, it buys freedom. Sometimes it buys imprisonment, even. Just ask the Hardhearts." He chuckled. "My fee was high on that one, but my father was more than happy to pay it…"

As he continued to jabber on, Count Malavic grinned delightedly like he'd just won the lottery. The fact that the audience was gaping in shock at him didn't slow down the goblin at all, and he continued to confess—unprompted—to what I was pretty sure amounted to financial crimes.

"Wow," said Liberty Freeman, looking more awkward than I'd ever seen him. "That's quite some, uh, clarity you have there, Orville."

"That's enough," Dante said. He marched past the other two judges and, before anyone could stop him, grabbed the vase from Orville. As the goblin blinked and looked around, Dante held the thing out at arm's length and marched back to the display table to set it down.

However, before he could release the burden, he said something that flipped my whole day upside down: "I'm in love with Dahlia."

Those who could hear him and knew us both seemed pleasantly surprised by the development. Sasha perked up and looked directly at me.

It was turning out to be a great day for the gossip hounds of Eastwind.

Instantly, I wished for those powers of invisibility. Had he really just said that? In front of everybody?

He'd never said "I love you" before. We weren't to that point, I didn't think. I felt strongly about him, and I certainly felt love for him, as I felt it for Grace or Nora, or even Tanner.

Dante and I had been dating for a while now, and I knew he liked me, but was he really *in love* with me? Had we known each other long enough for that to be possible?

"*Sweet baby jackalope,*" said Atlas. "*Did he just say…?*"

"*I don't know. Maybe I misheard.*"

"*Doubt it.*"

My face felt as hot as the sun, even though only those closest to Dante had heard his words, and most of the crowd was still focused on the main event: Orville.

While Dante had stemmed the flow of confessions from the goblin, he couldn't put the genie back in the bottle, and I'm not referring to Liberty Freeman.

Chaos erupted among the contestants.

Margot was shouting accusations, pointing at the elf Danny Shoehorn, who had his hands up, swearing he'd done no such thing as pay off a judge.

"Touch the vase and then try to deny it!" she shouted.

"How stupid do you think I am?" he snapped. "I'm not touching that cursed thing!"

"Everyone knows your family has more money than they know what to do with, smuggled away in Tearnanoch."

Amidst the hubbub, the wisp-thin young witch in thick-rimmed glasses that I'd assumed to be Orville's assistant appeared out of the crowd. She must've spotted her opportunity among the distraction, and she grabbed the goblin by the arm and expertly steered him away from the table and out of sight of the confrontation. I watched him disappear, wishing I could do the same but unable to take the action. I was far too lightheaded to do anything but concentrate on keeping my feet firmly planted on the ground as the emotions of the crowd tried to knock me this way and that. Loathing and shock and greed and excitement swirled around me like a tornado, rushing through me, making it difficult to remember where I ended and others began. I *was* the crowd. Or rather, the mob it was becoming.

"I didn't pay him anything!" Danny spat at Margot. "That glaze of yours is off. It makes people lie for no reason!"

More shouting, this time from the crowd. A powerful wave of envy hit my back, making me stumble forward, followed by a blast of schadenfreude that nearly took my feet out from under me. I wasn't sure if the crowd was closing in on me, threatening to crush me, or if it was *only* their emotions that were making it hard for me to breathe.

I felt something sharp and wet close in on my hand. I looked down. Atlas had my hand in his mouth, clasping it firmly but not aggressively in his teeth.

"Time to run away," he said. *"Hold on to my fur."*

Since my familiar was an expert at the flight part of fight-or-flight, I took his word for it. I couldn't do much thinking on my own anyway. Freeing myself of the toxic concoction of emotions flooding my body was as good a first step as any.

I gripped the shaggy white fur on the scruff of his neck and let him guide me toward liberation. But before I could feel the fresh spring breeze on my face, I cast a look over my shoulder and caught sight of Dante. Only later would I recognize how strange it was that he hadn't involved himself in the confrontation between Margot and Danny, even just to break it up. Instead, he stood by the entry table, hands in his pockets, staring right back at me. It felt as if he were about to holler something to me, but he said nothing, just watched me with a pained expression as I let Atlas lead me away. I don't remember what happened over the next few minutes, but that image of my boyfriend standing there, watching me run away, threatened to haunt me more than any restless spirit ever could.

Chapter Three

Grim was asleep on the couch when Atlas and I went inside. He roused immediately.

"You didn't go with Nora and Tanner?" I asked.

"Nope. Monster would get eaten in Wisconsin, so I'm cat-sitting her."

"Eaten! Ha!" The munchkin cat popped her head out of Grim's dark, shaggy fur. It was her default sleeping spot, and if I were as small as she was and had a best friend as big as Grim, I might do the same. It looked snuggly. *"Those beasties could try their best to eat me, but I'd fight my way out of their stomach. They'd be sorry!"*

I tried to keep a straight face, but her fierceness always seemed to clash adorably with her overwhelming cuteness. I wished I could say that Monster, Tanner's familiar, was all hiss and no claws, but she was both hiss and claws. That was why Atlas usually kept me between himself and her when we walked around the house, just like he was doing now, as we stood at the entrance to the living room. Monster never injured my familiar—I wasn't sure such a thing was even possible with the size differential and how Atlas's thick skin deflected her attempts at scratching him—but she had made a sport out of springing upon him from high surfaces, like countertops and the stairs, just to see him tuck tail and run. Poor boy. There wasn't much I could do about it, though, and at the end of the day, I hoped he'd get used to it and stop letting it affect him. Once he stopped giving her the reaction she wanted, she'd grow bored, maybe even cozy up to him like she had with Grim.

"*I thought you were gonna be at that dumb clay thing all day,*" Grim replied, yawning wide.

"It went south, unfortunately."

He perked up. "*And you didn't stick around to watch?*"

Atlas peeked around me. "*It was getting dangerous.*"

I scratched my familiar on the top of the noggin. "I was getting overwhelmed by the emotions and Atlas grabbed me and guided me out of there."

"*Oooh,*" said Monster mockingly. "*My hero.*"

"Hey, you," I said, wagging a finger at her, "don't discredit Atlas's bravery. He was a good boy."

Grim extended his legs forward in a big stretch. "*You gonna dish on the drama or what?*"

Atlas followed me over to the stuffed armchair across

from the couch, and as I settled in on it, he cautiously parked his rear end next to me, keeping an eye on the little furball in the big furball's coat.

I filled them in, starting with the lead-up to the judging.

"*Bor-ing!*" Grim declared. "*Get to the good part.*"

"I'm getting there," I said.

"*Not fast enough.*"

"*Start with when Raven picked up Margot's vase,*" Atlas suggested. "*That's when things started getting scary.*"

As I described Orville Ironhelm's confessions, both Grim and Monster laughed gleefully.

"*He just kept going?*" said Grim.

"Until Dante stepped in and took it away from him," I replied.

"*Killjoy,*" muttered Grim. "*Dante's too much of a good guy. What's with you Fifth Winds hooking up with these do-gooders? Ruby's the only one who can appreciate a bad boy.*"

Monster batted at the back of his head for insulting her witch, but Grim didn't seem to notice as another thought occurred to him. "*Hold on. If Dante took it from Orville, then he must've confessed something himself! Sweet baby jackalope, I hope it was something juicy.*"

"*It was,*" said Atlas, wagging his tail.

I felt my face heat up. "It was *not*. It was... It was personal."

Atlas wagged his tail some more, thudding the floorboards. *"He said he loved Dahlia."*

Monster gagged then coughed up a hairball. *"Ew."*

"Not this two-legged lovey-dovey stuff again," groaned Grim. *"The stifling pheromones nearly gave me permanent brain damage when Nora and Tanner were dating."*

I struggled to find the words. "It's not... We're not... I don't know if he meant—"

A knock on the front door saved me from explaining any of this to the peanut gallery, and I jumped up to answer it. Atlas followed on my heels.

Grace Merryweather was standing on my doorstep. "You okay?"

No "Hi, Dahlia!" or any such small talk from her, but that was to be expected. It was one of the things I appreciated about her as a friend. Straight into it.

"I'm fine."

"Oh, don't do that with me," she said. "Can I come in?"

I sighed. It was good to have a friend like Grace who didn't let me pull my usual tricks, but sometimes it was also a little frustrating. I liked using my usual tricks to avoid talking about the hard stuff. "Of course. Come on in. I'll make us some tea."

Grace regularly left her familiar at home, as most witches did. Nora, Ruby, and I were the only witches in town with canine familiars, and all the others had felines. Most cats preferred to be in the comfort of their home, and considering the per-capita of werewolves and other predators around town, I could see the logic in leaving the familiars where they were safe and sound.

I was especially grateful for it today; I didn't think I could deal with another furball's opinion on my dating life.

Grace didn't wait in the living room to be served. She followed me into the kitchen, and as I started the kettle, she went straight to the box of teas in the pantry and brought it out. Unlike Ruby True, whose tea setup I'd always found intimidating due to a lack of labeling, Nora and Tanner had their small boxes of tea clearly marked. I wasn't sure Grace would need that as badly as I would, since she was one of the smartest and most educated people I'd ever met, and could probably identify every ingredient by both sight and smell.

She scooped a green blend into two steeping pods and placed them in the mugs I'd pulled from the cabinet. "You ran out of there fast."

"I didn't run," I said. "Atlas dragged me."

"Too much emotion?"

I nodded. "I was starting to feel lightheaded."

"That's what I thought. Even I was feeling it, and you know I'm all in my head. I should've come to get you."

"No, no. You were all the way on the other side of the crowd and you had Monte with you." Monte was her five-year-old son. His biological father was a werewolf, and Monte was leaning that way so far in his development.

Landon Hawker, Grace's husband, had stepped up to raise him, and I couldn't think of better parents for a kid like Monte to have. They were patient with him, even as he took much longer than expected to begin forming full sentences. He lacked some fine motor skills too, but Grace and Landon dealt with things as they were, not as anyone thought they ought to be. She wasn't at all concerned about his delayed development, and was happy to meet him wherever it was. However, it did mean that Monte was a bit of a handful sometimes.

"He was with me, but so was Landon. He could've cared for him while I went and found you."

"Please don't beat yourself up," I said as the kettle whistled and I poured the water into our mugs. "All's well that ends well. I'm fine, and here we are, enjoying some tea in the peace and quiet." For Grace, who couldn't hear all the cross talk from the familiars, it really was a quiet house. For me, not so much.

I heard Grim shout from the living room, "*Stink bomb!*" and Monster cursing in protest.

Maybe we'd stay in the kitchen.

Grace cupped her mug in her hands and looked over the rim at me. "I spoke with Dante."

My stomach dropped. "Is he okay?"

She shrugged. "I think so. If not, he will be. You know how he is. I think he was a little disappointed about the judges' reaction to his teapot."

"That's not really what I meant." But it did occur to me that she was likely right, and rather than sticking around and comforting him, I'd split. Oof. Talk about being a bad friend, let alone girlfriend.

Grace inhaled the steam from her tea. "Mmm... I love this blend. Jasmine is my favorite." Then, switching gears in the way she always did, she said, "Was that the first time he said he loves you?"

I felt ashamed talking about this, even though I knew she wouldn't want me to feel that way. "Yes, it was. But does it even count?"

Grace arched a brow at me. "What in the realm do you mean by 'even count'?"

I stared down at the golden surface of my tea. "He didn't *mean* to say it. The clarity glaze made him do it."

"And?"

"Does that count if he wouldn't have said it otherwise?"

"Count for *what*, Dahlia?" she pressed.

I tried to find the words to make it make sense but ended up shrugging. "I don't know. It just seems like part of saying 'I love you' is that you decide you want to say it to someone, and then you say it."

Grace rolled her eyes. "I don't see why you're making this into some sort of formal mating ritual."

"I'm not!" I said, laughing.

"You are. *He's gotta say this in this context and mean it in this way, and then I have to respond with this to make it official.*"

"I never said that."

She cocked her head to the side. "Come on, Dahlia. It's been obvious to anyone with eyes that Dante loves you."

I blew absentmindedly on my tea. "Right, but that's not the same as being in love with someone."

"Sometimes it is. The two overlap."

"Would you say you're in love with me?" I asked.

She flashed me a grin. "Sure."

"Um."

"Does that make you uncomfortable? Oh, Dahl, come on. What does 'in love' even mean? I don't have romantic feelings for you. I'm in love with Landon. Then again, I only have romantic feelings for my husband *sometimes*. And other times I appreciate him deeply for the way he cares for our son. And other times still I feel like I'm going to have an aneurysm if I have to hear him do that little sniff he does every few seconds when he's reading a really engrossing text." She paused and leaned back against the counter. "You're trying to create all these boundaries and definitions for something that's amorphous and best left that way. So Dante said he's in love with you. He's been showing you how much he cares about you for months. The attention he gives you, the way he considers your needs before his own, how he keeps his word and stands up for you. No amount of saying 'I love you' or not changes any of that."

I frowned. "Maybe you're right."

"No, I *am* right. And I can tell that you love him, too."

I felt myself clam up.

"Don't you?" she prodded.

"Well, I suppose I have love for him, yes. But I don't know if I could say 'I love you' yet."

She narrowed her eyes at me over her mug. "You're still stuck on that. Huh. Okay, then. You don't have to say it back to him, especially if you don't mean it. But from simply observing the two of you, I'd say you're about as in love with each other as two people can be."

"Oh, stop it, Grace. You're making me self-conscious. Observing me like some wildlife biologist."

She shrugged. "You're the one creating all these strange mating rituals."

I laughed. "I wish you'd stop calling it that."

"Fine. Let's change the subject. How about those judges, huh?"

I was grateful to Grace for letting me off the hook and was more than happy to gossip about the many other interesting developments at the competition tent.

By the time we'd exhausted our recap, we'd switched to herbal tea, as it was getting on in the afternoon.

"Landon said he's fine taking Monte for the evening," she said, and I could almost hear their conversation where Landon knew I would need a friend for the evening and offered to do his part. "Wanna go grab an early dinner out? I'll need to bring Landon something home after."

"Not Monte?"

"No, he's only eating noodles and butter at the moment."

"Is that... okay?"

She shrugged. "It is what it is. You know, there's a part of me that wishes I could subsist off buttered noodles for a while. Add a dash of salt, maybe a little shredded cheese, and it's the solution to all of life's problems. Except malnutrition."

"Bring me and Monster something home, too," Grim chimed in from the other room. Eavesdropping, of course. Then again, what else was there to do as a lazy reincarnated hellhound whose witch was on vacation? At least he wasn't tearing anything up just because he could.

"Speaking of buttered noodles," continued Grace, "how does Franco's Pizza sound?"

When I hesitated, she laughed. "I'm kidding. I don't need you running into Dante right now. Not after he went and revealed the big shocker of being in love with you, something he only shows you every day."

I pinched her playfully on the arm, and she giggled and pulled away. "I could go for some soup and a sand-wich," I said. "Something light. And where the tourists aren't swarming. My stomach is still a little off after being in that crowd."

"Never mind," said Grim, and for a second I thought he was going to say he didn't need food—that would surely warrant concern. But then he continued, *"We're*

coming with you. Don't trust you to order the right thing, and we are hungry."

"*Starving,*" added Monster. "*I could eat an entire albino hellhound.*"

Atlas tucked his tail and hid behind me, and I wondered if I'd be lugging around these two for the entire weekend, or if my poor familiar could catch a break.

Chapter Four

Grim, Atlas, and Monster were snoozing beneath our table at Hagseed Café as Grace and I worked our way through a bottle of white wine for dessert. I'd ordered the hellhounds a plate of roast beef each, and Monster had attacked a small plate of tuna like it might escape.

I had no complaints about winding down the day this way. The restaurant was far enough from the center of town to avoid catching tired tourists wandering in, and it hadn't made Lot Flufferbum's infamous list of Eastwind's top restaurants—though it was quite good—and so it stayed off the itineraries of those visiting from Avalon.

An early dinner with my best friend, splitting a bottle of wine after a strange day that gave us lots to talk about—it didn't get much better than that, really. Maybe it was the alcohol, but the memory of Dante's confession was settling in my stomach less as a point of anxiety and more as the butterflies. Perhaps Grace had a point about it all. I still felt hesitant about the situation—after all, it was wrong to say "I love you" back to someone out of obligation and not because you really meant it. And I hadn't had enough time to really consider if I would mean it or not.

As Grace explained some interesting Eastwind history she'd read about in the most recent book she'd borrowed from the library, the evening took an unfortunate turn.

I caught a glimpse of him out of the corner of my eye. It almost didn't register to my brain, but then I did a double take.

Fangs and claws. It was Orville Ironhelm. He'd just entered the restaurant and was walking over.

Except he wasn't walking.

He was floating.

And while he'd entered through the front door of Hagseed Café, he hadn't actually opened it.

"Oh no," I muttered, causing Grace to pause in her retelling and look at me sideways.

"What is it?" she asked.

"Orville Ironhelm just showed up."

Not bothering with discretion one bit, she looked all around. "Where?"

The goblin arrived by our table, raised his chin to muster whatever dignity he could, and puffed out his chest. "Excuse me, miss," he said. "I have this strange tingling that you have the ability to see me. Is that correct?"

I nodded.

"Oh," said Grace, realizing why she was unable to spot him. "Ohhhh!"

Orville cleared his throat. "Then I would like for you to know that I'm dead."

"Yeah. Sorry about that," I replied.

"For fang's sake," muttered Grim. *"Not this again."*

I kept my attention on Orville's ghost. "And you need me to...?"

"Find my body," he finished for me. "I'm afraid it's unlikely to be discovered for hours otherwise, and I'd hate for it to stink by the time someone discovers it. Terribly undignified way to go."

I nodded and dabbed at my mouth with the napkin. "Got it." Turning to Grace, I said, "I gotta run."

"Oh no you don't," she said, hastily tossing a few coins on the table and then finishing the last of her wine. "Not without me."

"You don't have to," I assured her. "It probably won't be fun."

"It doesn't need to be *fun,*" she said. "It just needs to be interesting."

I glanced at Orville, the esteemed potter, the special guest in town, and the goblin who had just a few hours before confessed to various financial crimes. "I have a feeling it'll be *very* interesting."

Chapter Five

When we arrived at Cair Crestfall, the luxury hotel where Orville was staying for a few nights—though it looked like his stay in Eastwind might be extended now —I tried not to get distracted by the extravagance of the place.

I'd never been inside of Cair Crestfall, but I knew it was for the wealthier guests and tourists to the realm. I had no idea just how ornate and spacious it would feel, though. It even smelled immaculate, with a whisper of lily greeting my nostrils the second we stepped into the high-ceilinged lobby.

I couldn't imagine that Eastwind needed a hotel this big and expensive prior to the recent tourist boom. Before that, had these rooms stayed empty? Or was I so out of touch with the upper crust that I didn't realize how many wealthy individuals came and went from town?

The hotel was located in the expensive shopping district, which was hardly more than a single street branching out a few blocks away from Fulcrum Park. I never came this way since I couldn't afford Echo Chambers' expensive salon or Atlantis Day Spa or any of the high-end shopping that was offered. Even if I *could* afford it, I wouldn't know what to do with such decadent things... though it might be nice to see what a well-trained stylist could do with this curly hair of mine.

The sun had almost disappeared completely behind the horizon by the time we arrived, yet the interior of the lobby was well lit with floating orbs of soft light, the kind I'd grown used to in Eastwind with its lack of electricity. Nothing needed electricity here; everything ran on magic.

My boots clacked over the marble floors of the lobby as Grace and I passed the modern leather couches and gently bubbling water feature to approach the front desk. Atlas and Grim (with Monster on his back) padded behind us. I was always amazed by how such big beasts could move so silently. Bad luck for any of their natural prey in the Deadwoods. However, neither Grim nor Atlas had to hunt anymore since they'd paired up with their witch. Instead, they tagged along and got full plates of roast beef. Domestication wasn't so bad.

The hotel clerk looked up as we approached. He had a round and youthful face covered in freckles and thick curls atop his head.

Oh, and small horns.

The rectangular name tag on his shirt read *Ferin*.

"Welcome to Cair Crestfall!" His attention darted quickly to the furry tagalongs, and for a second I thought he was going to explain the hotel's pet policy. Instead he returned his attention to me and smiled. "What can I help you with this evening?"

I drummed my fingertips on the front desk, trying to figure out how to word it. "Um, well, my name's Dahlia Wildes, and—"

His eyes went wide. "The Fifth Wind witch?"

Oh right. Everyone knew my name in town, even if they didn't know me. The perk of being a death witch. My reputation preceded me. Yay for lingering stigma.

"Yes," I said, forcing a smile. "That's me. So, I'm here —we're here—because we believe you might have a situation on your hands..."

Grace stepped up beside me. "One of your guests died."

The clerk, Ferin, stared at her. "I'm sorry?"

Orville's ghost groaned beside me. "Fauns really are dimwitted creatures, aren't they?"

I ignored that bit of bigotry and tried to keep up with the conversation. "I believe one of your guests" —I leaned over the desk to avoid being overheard, even though the rest of the lobby was empty—"Orville Ironhelm has died."

Ferin's brows pinched together. "And how would you— Oh. Oh! Is he... here?"

"Yes, he's here." I motioned to my left, where he was floating impatiently.

Louder than was necessary, since the goblin was dead, not deaf, Ferin said, "I am so sorry to hear your stay at Cair Crestfall has not lived up to your expectations, Mr. Ironhelm." He scrunched up his nose and lowered his voice. "I shouldn't use the word 'lived.' That's offensive." He turned to me. "Isn't it?"

"Quite," said Orville, "though it's the least offensive thing about him."

Oh boy. "I think it's fine," I said, reassuring the clerk so that he might continue helping us. "The sentiment is appreciated. But maybe you could send someone to Mr. Ironhelm's room to check on him?"

Ferin swallowed hard. "Was he... Will it be, um, bloody?"

I honestly hadn't thought about that. I turned to Orville, who said, "No, no. Quite clean."

"It's clean. Nothing too scary," I said, hoping the ghost could be believed.

Ferin nodded. "Then I'll go check on it myself." He didn't look too excited about the prospect, and I wondered if he'd ever seen a dead body before. My first time had certainly been a shock. The stillness of death is apparent, even from a distance. You don't realize how much even a sleeping body moves until you encounter one that doesn't move at all.

Not wanting to put the round-faced faun through that, I said, "You know what? Let's just call in Deputy

Manchester. I'm sure he would be happy to have an uncontaminated scene, just in case it turns out that it's not, well, due to natural causes."

The relief was clear on Ferin's face. "I'll send an emergency owl."

As he disappeared, Orville sighed. "Homicide? What a shame that would be. A death reserved for commoners and crooks. How embarrassing!"

Chapter Six

I didn't register how quickly things were happening regarding Orville's death until Deputy Manchester arrived on scene and slowed it all to a grinding halt. When I thought about it, that was likely intentional on Stu's part. Better to be slow and meticulous now to avoid regretting it later. Once evidence was lost, it was lost.

Still, the eventful day was making it hard for me to keep my eyes open as I waited for news on a stiff leather couch. Grace had already excused herself to grab dinner for Landon and Monte before it got too late, and so it was just me and the familiars waiting with Orville in the airy lobby of the hotel until it was clear Stu didn't need me for anything.

You might have a glamorized idea of what it means to be a witch who can see ghosts and help solve crimes, but the truth is that a lot of it turns out to be little more than waiting around.

I tried to make myself useful, or at least keep myself awake, by getting whatever information I could from Orville about the events leading up to his death, but if he remembered much of those final moments, which spirits sometimes didn't—death could be traumatic—he wasn't interested in sharing them with me.

Orville provided no useful information, in fact, and I quickly found myself preferring he would stop talking entirely. He was entirely concerned with how his fellow aristocrats would judge his death, especially following on the heels of his recent confessions, which he claimed were "complete fictions."

"The glaze was faulty, most definitely," he prattled on. "Whatever chemical mix that witch concocted was a mess. A clarity glaze? Ha! More like a lie inducer. A scandal squeezer. Not a word of what I uttered was true. I would never accept a bribe. I don't need it. When you're as successful and renowned of a potter as I am, people throw sacks of gold at you! Why would I need to accept bribes? Bah! Preposterous."

At first, as was my nature, I listened along and considered his claims. Maybe the glaze *didn't* force confessions but elicited lies to cause chaos. It was possible. Magic was, for lack of a better word, *weird* like that.

But the longer he protested, the more I began to believe he was protesting *too much*.

I can't tell you how relieved I was when Ted walked through the lobby doors.

"So we meet again, Dahlia!"

I waved to him as he approached and couldn't help but notice that it sounded more like he was walking across dried leaves than an expensive marble floor. "I suppose it's true what they say," I replied playfully, "you can't escape death."

"Heh. So true. Hold on, do they say that? Are people trying to escape me?" He sounded genuinely dismayed.

"No, no," I said, "not like that. It's just a saying." I shook my head. "I don't even know why people say it. I mean, I guess death comes for us all."

"Not everyone," he said with a shrug. "Some of my best friends are immortal. Technically, so am I."

I let out a big breath. "Right. Of course. Sometimes I forget I'm in Eastwind. I'm sorry, I'm tired. It's been a long day."

Ted took a seat on the leather couch across from mine, his bones rattling as he lowered himself onto it. "Wanna talk about it?"

"I would," I said, "but I feel like I've talked and talked about it already. Thanks for offering, though."

"Of course. You know I have nothing but time. Heh." He turned his attention to Orville, who appeared insulted by his protestations being cut off by the arrival of a reaper. "You're the dead guy, right? I'm Ted. I'll be cleaning up your body today and ushering you into the great beyond. What's your name?"

Orville raised his chin and floated higher so that he was looking down on Ted where the reaper hunched casually in his mass of black robes. "My name is Orville

Ironhelm, master potter, heir to the Ironhelms of East-wind, and known throughout Avalon as a goblin of incredible taste and skill."

Ted gave him a gloved thumbs-up. "Cool."

In what felt like a pretty reckless move to me, considering his disembodied situation, Orville scowled at the reaper. "It's more than *cool*."

Ted laid his scythe across his lap so he could give Orville a double thumbs-up. "You're right. It's *awesome sauce*."

Orville appeared so offended he might blink out of existence at that very moment.

But Ted didn't seem to notice. "Did Deputy Manchester say if it seemed like natural causes or foul play yet?"

I shook my head. "Still waiting for something."

Ted wagged a playful finger at Orville. "Then I guess you'd better stay right here until we figure that out. Can't usher you to the other side if you might have important information to help with a murder investigation. Heh."

"I doubt he does," I said. "I've already asked him if he remembers how he died. He said he was drinking his afternoon tea, got sleepy, lay down, and that was the last thing he remembers. I asked him to give me more details and he started talking about how squeaky clean his reputation is." I rolled my eyes.

"Regardless of the deputy's findings," said Orville, "I have no desire to let you usher me to *the great beyond*, whatever questionable place that is."

I looked from the spirit to the reaper. "Can he do that? Just say he won't go?"

Ted nodded cheerfully, a sound of rattling bones accompanying the gesture. I actually found it quite a pleasant sound, up there with the clip-clopping of horse hooves on cobblestone.

"I definitely want consent from the spirits," he explained. "It's important to their journey. Sometimes they withhold it... for a while. They always come around." He paused. "Well, not *always*. Heh. If they've been murdered and it goes unsolved, they can hang around indefinitely. Any unfinished business can keep them from consenting, really, though I can usually convince them to let it go over time. The main exception is when their unfinished business is a thirst for knowledge. A thirst for knowledge can sometimes become unquenchable. In that case, I usually show them over to the library. Once they read all the books there, which can take a long, long time depending on their reading speed, they usually find me and I show them the way on. It's silly, actually, because if they'd just let me take them to the other side, they'd instantly be provided all the answers to their questions! But I guess there's something to be said for learning things on your own."

The sound of boots stomping down the grand staircase announced Deputy Stu Manchester's arrival into the lobby. I'd worked with Stu on a couple of murder investigations, and I'd developed a real soft spot for the man. In his early fifties, Stu was a perpetual bachelor, due in part to the hours his job required. He was one of the most courteous and committed people in this town, though, always professional, always polite. I did occasionally sense a simmering sadness beneath his congenial demeanor, but I didn't think we were close enough for me to ask about it. I hated to prod on things like that, since it was often private and not everyone was open to talking about their feelings.

Stu was a were-elk, and I'd seen him in that form only once. In his human form, he was a little on the tall side, with a bristly mustache and a belly that spoke of his years eating a big slice of Tanner's famous cherry pie at the diner after each shift. I loved that little indulgence for an otherwise by-the-book man like him.

He stopped at the bottom of the staircase, looked at Ted and me as he hitched up his duty belt, and said, "You can probably come collect him now, Ted."

"You sure?" asked the reaper.

"Didn't see anything right away that would indicate foul play. Now, considering some of the magic in this town, I can't completely rule it out. But it seems likely that his heart stopped suddenly. Congenital defect, or what have you."

Stu looked tired, which might've explained his playing a little fast and loose with information that felt like it should be proprietary.

"Are you okay?" I asked.

He furrowed his brow. "Huh?"

"You seem... tired."

Stu dragged a hand over his face. Though he usually kept his bristle mustache clean and concise, there was currently stubble growing in on his chin. "Didn't get much sleep last night."

"Oh no!" said Ted. "Why's that?"

Stu looked back and forth between the reaper and me. "Um. Well. Just a little anxious, I guess."

"About what?" asked Ted.

The deputy didn't look used to being the one on this side of the interview. "Nothing."

"Oh, come on, Stu," Ted prodded. "Anxiety is meant to be spoken aloud. That's how it goes away! It's nothing to be ashamed about."

I kept my mouth shut, fearing that if I said anything, it would prevent the deputy from opening up.

"I guess... It's been a while since I was the only deputy available. With Deputy Culpepper out of town for the weekend, it's bringing back those memories. In my chest." He placed a palm over his sternum. "Not sure what it's about, really. I used to work this job on my own with only occasional help from Sheriff Bloom for years and years. Now I have a weekend on my own and I can't sleep?" He shook his head. "Maybe I'm just getting too old for this job."

"I dunno," I said, "it sounds like maybe you never realized how much stress you were under before. That doesn't mean you're weak now, or too old for the job. It could simply mean you asked too much of yourself before."

"Or the town asked too much of you," said Ted. He reached to put a comforting hand on the deputy's shoulder, but stopped short of actually touching him to avoid adding a death chill to Stu's anxiety. "I gotta say, you really stepped up. You held it together for *years* with only occasional help from Sheriff Bloom and Ruby True. You ought to be proud of that."

Stu nodded but stared at the marble floor. "Maybe so. Let's just hope that when we get Mr. Ironhelm to the medical examiner, he confirms that it's a death by natural cause. Don't need a homicide investigation on my hands this weekend on top of the usual policing."

"It's probably nothing," said Ted, dropping his arm to his side.

"Well." I'd said it before I could stop myself. I didn't want to be the bearer of bad news, but Orville *was* still hovering around.

Stu looked at me. "You know something, Miss Wildes?"

Grimacing apologetically, I said, "Orville's ghost is hanging around. Doesn't that usually mean he was murdered?"

"Sometimes," said Ted. "But not always."

"And then there was this drama he was involved in earlier today. Public drama. I could see it making someone mad enough to at least attack him."

Stu took a deep breath, then straightened his shoulders and, with what seemed like great effort, said, "Okay, then. Let's hear about this."

I filled him in on it, despite Orville's trying to correct the record every five seconds in ways that made him look much less like a financial criminal. I stuck with my recollection, though. It seemed important to do so.

"That's certainly something that could get a few people riled up," Stu concluded. "If only Deputy Culpepper were here. He has this thing he can do with his wand where he scans for traces of magic on scene. That's not something you can do, is it?"

I cringed apologetically. "No. I'm not a useful kind of witch."

"Come on now," said Ted supportively, as Stu added, "I wouldn't say that, Miss Wildes."

"You're incredibly useful!" the reaper continued. "Besides, the measure of a person isn't their *use*."

I smiled at him. "Thanks, Ted."

Stu stroked fingers over his mustache. "However, if you *wanted* to be of some use, I would obviously appreciate the help this weekend."

"Of course. What can I do?"

"Keep talking to Mr. Ironhelm. See if he remembers anything new. I'll treat this as a possible homicide until we can hear back from both the medical examiner and the magical examiner and they rule it out. I'll ask the clerk to keep the room locked and not clean it, in case we need to check for spells and the like later on. Would you be up for helping in that way?"

I'd had anxiety on and off for my whole life, and I was currently attached to a highly anxious familiar, so I had nothing but compassion for anyone who was struggling with it. There was no question of whether I would help Stu now that he'd asked me to. For one, I would want other people to do the same for me, but mostly, I could tell he wasn't used to asking for help. I didn't want to discourage his early attempts at it. "Totally. If I can get anything useful out of Orville, I'll let you know."

Stu nodded. "And I'll let you know when I hear more about the body, in case that jogs his memory at all."

"I question the quality of his memory to start with, so —" I looked around for the ghost, expecting him to debate me on that fact, but he was nowhere to be seen.

"What is it?" asked Stu.

I forced a smile. "He's disappeared. But I'm sure he'll turn up. And when he does, I'll have another conversation with him."

And we would just have to hope that it was more productive and honest than any of the ones I'd had with him so far.

Chapter Seven

I realized after the fact that the hotel clerk, Ferin, had been listening in on our conversation from his place behind the check-in desk. Once Stu had returned to the scene of the death to look for any further clues, the faun approached Ted and me to offer us some complimentary tea in the hotel's tearoom. Neither one of us was silly enough to turn that down in a place this nice. It was late, sure, but I knew that after a day this strange I wouldn't be falling right to sleep as soon as my head touched the pillow.

Besides, I enjoyed Ted, and not many people did. It felt like a privilege to spend time with him without the creep of my own mortality getting to me like it did most everyone else. Behind the scythe and reminder of mortality was a kindhearted and generous person. It occurred to me that it might be *because* of his continuous contact with death that he was so lovely, not despite it.

Grim, Atlas, and Monster joined us, but settled into a spot in the corner of the tearoom, where they'd spread out large beds for any visiting witch's familiar to make itself cozy. (I promised that I would get them each a treat for being good and not overturning any of the delicate tables in the cramped but expensive space.)

"Poor Stu," said Ted, as a pixie flitted up to the table to pour our tea. While I'd gone with an herbal lavender tea, Ted had opted for a black breakfast tea that would've kept me up for hours longer than I already would be. I sometimes wondered where the tea, or any food and beverage, went in him, since his face was obscured by his hood and he rattled like he was made of nothing but bones. My working theory was that beneath his cloak and gloves was little more than a skeleton, but I wouldn't go so far as to say there was flesh. I supposed it wasn't worth wondering too much about, though. For one, it was really none of my business how his body worked. But for another, the fact that he was the was a grim reaper moved the whole conversation outside of the realm of normal biological composition right off the bat.

The pixie flitted away silently after pouring the hot water into our cups to steep, and returning my attention to Ted's initial comment, I replied, "You mean the anxiety?"

"Exactly. I didn't know he struggled with it. I care about him. How could I not have known?"

"Some people are good at hiding it. Maybe not on purpose, but to be able to keep functioning. And it can look all kinds of different ways, or so I've read. Have you ever struggled with it?" I asked.

"Me? Not in the normal sense. Never had anxiety about dying or aging or any of that. Heh. But sometimes I feel anxious about people."

"Social anxiety," I said.

He nodded. "Yeah, I guess it's that. Heh. Have you experienced anxiety before?"

I chuckled. "Looking back, I think I've experienced every type of anxiety there is."

"Really? You seem so calm, though."

"Do I?" It certainly never felt that way on the inside.

"You do. It's hard to tell what you're feeling sometimes."

"Huh. That's a bit ironic."

He sipped his tea, which was still scalding hot, then said, "Why's that?"

"Because one of my powers is that I can sense other people's emotions. I can tell what they're feeling even when I don't want to."

Rather than withdrawing, like I expected most people to, Ted perked up. "That's neat! Can you tell what I'm feeling right now?"

"Sure, but it's only from the tone of your voice. You're one of the few people in Eastwind whose emotions my powers don't pick up on."

Ted nodded, his hood rippling gently. "Not surprised. I'm impervious to most magic. Sort of part of the gig. Can't be influenced by magic when I have such an important job and I'm the only one in town who can do it. For what it's worth, it would be okay if you read my emotions. I don't mind, and I trust you."

The gratitude I felt was all my own. "That means a lot, Ted. And if you don't mind keeping it between us that I have that power..."

He held up a gloved hand. "Say no more. I know all about having powers that freak people out. Speaking of which, do you reckon Orville was murdered?"

I nibbled on the inside of my lip as I tapped into the suspicions that had been forming in the back of my mind since he dropped in at the café. "I hate to be cynical, but I do think it's a possibility," I replied. "The timing seems suspicious, doesn't it?"

"All those things he was confessing at the pottery competition sure do sound like motive for *someone*. Then again, it's possible that he was so anxious about having confessed publicly that he went back to his room and had a heart attack or something."

That was an interesting theory. "You think a guilty conscience might've killed him?"

"Wouldn't be the first time," Ted replied.

It clicked for me in that moment that Ted was likely a treasure trove of death statistics relevant to Eastwind. After all, anyone who'd died here and moved on had spent their last ghostly moments walking alongside him. He was certainly a useful expert to have on hand in a murder investigation... if that was what this turned into.

"I hate to even suggest it," said Ted, "but do you

think Orville might've taken his own life? Out of shame or to avoid consequences for what he confessed?"

I respected the suggestion by taking time to consider it, even though my gut—or perhaps that was the Insight that Nora kept telling me about—gave me back a hard no. "Orville strikes me as the type of person who assumes he won't be met with consequences. Besides that, I think he loves himself too much to disgrace his name that way."

"Fair enough," Ted said. "From the little I know of him, he doesn't remind me of the people I know who went that way. They usually feel bad for what they've done."

"Exactly, and he won't even admit that he's done it. Outside of apparently being compelled to, assuming that's what was going on with the clarity glaze."

We fell into a comfortable silence, and I used the opportunity to try my lavender tea. I narrowly avoided moaning the moment the calming floral scent wafted into my nostrils. It was a little chilly in the tearoom, and the warmth of the drink was like being wrapped up in a comforting hug. For a few moments, I forgot all about the dead goblin.

"Good?" said Ted.

"Very good." I set down the cup so I didn't go straight through it. As strange as it sounds, there was little that made me more forlorn than getting to the end of a tasty warm beverage. "I hate to take it this direction," I said, "but maybe for the duration of our teatime we could assume that Orville was murdered and think through some of the suspects or people to interview."

"Ooh, I like that."

"And if by the end of the conversation we decide that it's unlikely there was any foul play or we can't come up with a solid motive for murder, we'll assume it was natural causes until Stu lets us know otherwise."

"I like this game already," said Ted.

It did feel much less bleak to call it a game, so I went with that.

I looked around the tearoom, making sure the decedent's ghost hadn't reappeared to eavesdrop or chime in with more unhelpful self-promotion. He was nowhere to be found, so I dove in. "Who doesn't like Orville Ironhelm?"

"From what you've said about the competition, there are probably a few people who are unhappy with him right now."

"True. Margot really wanted to win, and he came right out and said she would if it weren't for his already being bribed by Danny Shoehorn."

"Then Danny probably isn't too happy with him, either, being exposed that way."

"True," I said. "And I hate to even mention it, but Raven is probably upset about this whole thing. She spent a lot of money to get Orville to come, apparently, and he sort of blew the whole thing up."

Ted nodded slowly, but said, "I don't see Raven murdering anyone."

"Me neither."

"There is one other person who might not be the biggest fan of Orville Ironhelm," said Ted apprehensively. "I'm not saying he did it, but over the years, I *have* heard him say some spiteful things about the Ironhelms."

I tried to follow along, but my brain was tired. "Who is this?"

"The person sitting next to Orville at the table."

"Count Malavic?" I was less shocked that Malavic would want to kill someone and more shocked that the animosity had been right in front of my eyes, and I hadn't picked up on it sooner.

"I'm not saying Sebastian did it," said Ted quickly. "Definitely not saying that. Heh. He's my friend. But I do think he'd be someone to talk to. Sometimes, when people hold grudges against a person or family, they become amateur biographers on the target."

"Biographers who keep track of the unflattering bits to build their case against the person," I said.

Ted chuckled. "Right. But rolling with the possibility that Orville was murdered, those unflattering things are the facts that could shed the most light on a motive and suspect." He held up his gloved hands. "And again, I'm not saying Sebastian did it. Yes, he has a grudge, but I've known him for a long time, and he's capable of holding on to many grudges at a time without letting any take control of him. One of the learned skills of being an immortal, heh."

I wasn't thrilled at the prospect of speaking to Malavic, not after all the warnings Nora had given me about the vampire. "If I do go speak with him, would you...?"

"Say no more. Of course. I'll go with you. I'm always thrilled for a chance to see my friends! Maybe we can meet at the pub and get a game of scufflepuck in while we're there."

Sheehan's Pub had the only public scufflepuck boards in town, and Malavic and Ted could often be found there, playing as a pair, and wiping the floor with whoever challenged them. Malavic and Ted had the obvious unfair advantage of most likely being around when the game was first invented, so it wasn't a huge surprise that they tended to win. The only time they *didn't* was when Ted was clearly throwing the game to keep his competitors from being too hard on themselves.

I'd once overheard at the pub that Tanner and Donovan were a formidable team in their younger years, but Tanner hardly had time to play with his job as a deputy sheriff, and Donovan was, well, in a completely different and detached realm now (and doing great, I happened to know).

"Who else would be worth talking to?" Ted asked.

"Orville, if he ever gives us anything useful." My mind flashed back to the kerfuffle at the competition, right before Atlas led me away. The young witch had come and extricated Orville. "I think he has an assistant.

Or an agent, maybe? Someone who works with him. I saw her at the competition, and she pulled him away when things got contentious. I didn't recognize her from Eastwind. It was clear he knew her, though. Maybe she saw something."

"Or maybe she... you know," said Ted.

"Maybe. But we don't know anything about her. Means, motive, and opportunity, Ted. We don't know that she had any of those yet. We don't even know who she is. First things first."

Ted chuckled. It was a dry sound, like bones over a chalkboard, but I quite liked it. "You're becoming such a good sleuth! Nora must be training you well. She's a very good investigator. I've seen her work. She's put herself in some truly dangerous situations for a mortal. Eastwind is lucky to have her. I think we're lucky to have you, too! I don't mean to give her all the credit for your talents and hard work."

"No, it's fine. She deserves most of the credit. I'm not nearly as brave as she is, either, so don't get your hopes up about my potential."

"If I called Nora brave to her face, *she'd* deny it, too." He sipped his tea. "Anyone else we should talk to?"

"I was thinking... perhaps the clerk saw something. Ferin. Orville must've come in through the lobby before he died. Was he with anyone? Did he look ill then? Did he say anything? What was his mood?"

"Ooh, that's a good idea. He seemed like a nice guy. I bet he'll be helpful."

"Would you like to come with me to speak with him?" I asked.

Ted lowered his head. "It does sound like you have a lot of work ahead of you this weekend, and I'm sure you'd rather spend the time with Dante than investigating a murder that might not even be a murder, but... people don't like talking to me." He sighed. "I could never be a sleuth because of that."

"*I* like talking to you, Ted!" I protested. "And I need you to come with me to speak with Malavic. He's your friend, so he might tell you things he wouldn't tell me. And if he lies, you'd be more likely to spot it than I would."

That seemed to cheer him up. "Of course. Now, Sebastian doesn't lie all that much. I should say that. He's not a liar, per se. He doesn't have to. He can usually tell the truth and get away with things. And at the end of the day, I do think he has the realm's best interests at heart."

I decided not to debate that point. Ted knew the vampire way better than I did, anyway.

He went on, "But he *does* stretch the truth sometimes, and I'm usually pretty good at calling him on it. That's what friends do, right? Hold each other accountable."

"I like that," I said, before the memory of Dante confessing his love for me sprang to mind followed by... my running away. I ought to reach out to him. If I were in his position, I'd be losing my mind wondering if I'd screwed up. I needed to reach out.

As soon as I knocked out a little bit of this investigation, I would do just that.

Not yet. But soon. Probably.

Chapter Eight

Ted left to check in with Deputy Manchester as I approached the front desk of the hotel. Behind me, Grim and Monster wrestled by the couches, while Atlas stayed close by my side. Ferin was perched behind a large open ledger, reading a book. As I approached, I was able to read the title on the cover. *Boundaries for Beginners.* His curls bobbed about his face as he jerked his head up to greet me. "Dahlia. Anything I can help you with?"

"Yes, actually."

He straightened, slipped a leather bookmark in the pages, then set the book quickly aside, staring eagerly at me, his hooves clip-clopping gently against the marble floors.

"I think you might be a key witness," I said.

His eyes went wide. "You think it was a murder?"

"No, no," I said, realizing that I was probably

bringing that mindset into this conversation with me, and it might not be the most useful in getting to the truth. "Did you see Orville Ironhelm when he arrived earlier this afternoon, just after lunchtime?"

"He walked right there." Ferin traced the route from the front doors to the stairs with a finger.

"And was he with anyone?" I asked.

"Yes, his assistant was with him."

I tried not to get too excited. "His assistant? Was she a younger witch?"

He nodded.

"And do you know her name?"

"I— I'm not sure if I should give that out to you."

I didn't let that deter me. "Why? Is she a guest here?"

"Oh, horns. Yeah, she is. I didn't mean for you to know that, either." He sighed, his round face drooping.

"It's okay," I assured him. "No one needs to know about our conversation outside of you and me, okay?"

He swallowed and lifted his chin again.

"*I smell a lot of fear on this guy,*" said Atlas. "*Wonder what he's so afraid of.*"

That was a good question. At first, I'd assumed he was just a little awkward, maybe intimidated by the presence of multiple hellhounds. But he'd hardly looked at Atlas when we approached the desk this time. Something else regarding this situation was possibly making him nervous.

"Can you describe the woman who was with him? What was she wearing? How was she acting?"

"I don't know that I'd even call her a woman. She was young, like you said. But she had thick glasses, was quite thin, and she was sort of... holding him up. Not completely. He could walk on his own, I'm pretty sure, and I'm not sure she was strong enough to hold him up, but she was hunched over him, attending to him."

That made sense. He was probably distraught, and I wouldn't be surprised if he had some physical symptoms along with that. Also, if we were talking about the same witch, she was significantly taller than the goblin, so hunching came with that territory.

"Was she saying anything to him?" I asked.

"Not that I could hear. She was sort of... muttering to him. It sounded calming, though, like a mother would croon to a crying baby."

"And they both went upstairs together?"

He nodded.

I hated to even go there, but I had to ask. "And they had... separate rooms?"

"Oh yes!" he said, laughing. Then he stopped himself short. "I probably shouldn't've given out that information."

"There's that fear again," said Atlas.

"I'm glad you did," I replied to Ferin, not my familiar. "It helps me to know what the, um, relationship between them was."

"From what I could tell, it was only professional. She looks young enough to be his granddaughter."

I offered a smile. "That's a relief, then. Did she stay upstairs once she brought him up?"

"Oh! I do know that. No, she went up with him and came right back down."

Interesting. "How did she look when she came down after?"

He paused, gazing toward the ceiling as he recalled. "Frustrated? No, not quite that. Maybe a little annoyed. Tired. I used to have this grandfather, and every time we visited him, he would tell me how I needed to get a good job, have some faun pride, and on and on. Never satisfied with me. I left his house every time feeling the way she looked."

"And has she returned to the hotel since she left?"

He cringed. "Um. Well. I'm not sure. I took a late lunch break. Around two in the afternoon. It may have run a little longer than usual."

"*Fear's back,*" said Atlas, but he didn't need to keep telling me; I could feel it shoot off the faun in bursts any time he seemed to believe he'd fallen down on the job.

"That's okay," I said. "No crime in taking your lunch."

His face twisted with anguish. "Oh, but I shouldn't have done it. I should've brought lunch with me. Instead, I just stuck a sign up saying when I'd be back. It was probably during my lunch break that he was killed, wasn't it?"

"We don't know the time yet, *and* we don't know that he was killed. He could've passed in his sleep."

"He wasn't that old for a goblin."

Having no idea about any of that, I took his word for it. "Sometimes people die young. Listen, Ferin, it's very important that you don't blame yourself for this. I'm a salesclerk at the pottery shop, and I leave for lunch breaks sometimes, too. I put up a sign to let people know when I'll be back, and nothing bad comes of it."

"Please don't tell the owner. He'll find a way to blame me. He's always going on about how impossible it is to find good help in the hospitality industry. And he... he scares me sometimes."

The fear pulsed off him more than ever now.

"I won't tell the owner," I assured him. "Out of curiosity, though, who owns the hotel?"

He hesitated, then his shoulders slumped. "It's not a secret, I suppose. Public records." With a deep breath, he managed to muster the name. "The Count."

"Count Malavic?" I said, blinking.

He nodded.

"That'll do it," said Atlas, tucking his tail slightly.

On the one hand, it was interesting to hear that name come up again. If Malavic had a grudge against the Iron-helms, and one of them had been found dead in a hotel that he owned...

On the other hand, it wasn't all that surprising. Malavic recently became the owner of what was formerly called the Muscoff Manor Inn, now the Malavic Manor Inn, and there'd been a death there as well. I'd investigated that one fully and it was clear enough that Malavic had nothing to do with it. Perhaps he was just unlucky in which businesses he owned. Or perhaps he owned so many businesses in this town that if someone died outside their home, the odds heavily favored it taking place on one of his properties. I'd have to look into all that, but it was certainly interesting to discover that he was the owner of Cair Crestfall.

"He's a good boss," Ferin continued. "I don't want you to think I'm ungrateful for him hiring me on. He didn't have to. I'd never worked in hospitality. But he brought me on as soon as he bought this place."

I arched a brow. "Did that happen recently?"

"About three months ago."

"Any idea who owned it before him?"

"I have a pretty good guess. Some of the paperwork from the old owners is still in the drawers back here. I wasn't trying to snoop, but when I was searching for other things—"

I held up a hand. "I believe you. You don't seem like the snooping type. Don't worry. Who owned this place before the Count?"

"I don't know *exactly*," he said. "It was a trust or something like that. The Ironhelm Trust." The color drained from his face. "Wait. Ironhelm."

A lot had happened over the last few hours, so I didn't judge him for being late in making the connection.

"I knew I recognized the name," said Ferin. "On the reservation. Ironhelm."

"And you're sure your brain isn't mixing up the two

names? Like maybe it was the Steelhelm Group or something?"

He shook his head as he pulled open one of the drawers on his side of the reception desk. After rifling through, he held up a piece of paper triumphantly. On it was scribbled a bunch of handwritten notes that weren't immediately legible, but at the top was a clear header with a crest. Sure enough, *The Ironhelm Trust* was printed clearly at the top.

"Wow," I said.

"Right?"

"May I see that?"

He handed it over. "Can't be confidential since they don't own this place anymore, right?"

Sure, I'd go with that. But as it turned out, the writing on the page wasn't particularly interesting, either. It looked like a jumble of notes made by whomever manned the front desk prior to the transfer of ownership. Things like, *towels rm109* and *request holiday vacay hrs.* It all appeared to be in the same scrawling handwriting, and none of it seemed particularly relevant to why a goblin was dead upstairs.

The header, though, now that was interesting. The Ironhelm Trust.

"I'm going to ask you one more question, Ferin, and I know it's going to make you uncomfortable, so if you don't want to tell me, I'm happy to grab Deputy Manchester to come ask you in an official capacity."

I felt the tension rising inside him, so I just went for it.

"Did Orville Ironhelm pay for his own room?"

Ferin pressed his lips together on impulse, and I knew there was something important there.

"Listen, Count Malavic is a friend of mine," I said, only being partially dishonest. "I've worked with him before. I know you're worried about getting in trouble with him, but if he tries to fire you, I'll make sure he doesn't. And Ted, who was in here earlier? Probably the Count's *best* friend, and one of the nicest people you'll meet. He'll stand up for you, too. Can you please just tell me if Orville paid for his room? Just a yes or no?" I tried to put on some feminine wiles with an innocent smile, though I wasn't working with much, and I couldn't necessarily assume he was susceptible to that. It was worth a shot, though.

Yuck, no. It wasn't me. I dropped the act. "Ferin, please. Did he pay for his own room?"

I doubt the clerk realized that he was tapping his hoof nervously.

He shook his head.

"Do you know who paid for it?" I asked.

He shook his head again, his fear so strong I could almost taste it.

"*He's locking up,*" said Atlas. "*I recognize the signs.*"

If anyone was an expert on the freeze response to fear, it would be my familiar. I had to accept that pushing would only make things worse.

I had plenty of interesting information to mull over as it was, though, so I thanked Ferin for his time, and Atlas and I left him at the desk.

Why was Malavic's name coming up so much already? Could it all be coincidence, or was there a deeper plot running through the town that I was on the precipice of unearthing?

Chapter Nine

Orville's young assistant was standing with Deputy Manchester when I walked upstairs. Her eyes were swollen from crying, and she kept lifting her glasses to rub at them.

Stu cast me a glance when I approached. I'd seen that look on many a man who was faced with a distraught woman he didn't quite know what to do with. No doubt the deputy had lots of practice dealing with crying people in his line of work, but she was beyond that, bawling her eyes out and shaking.

As I approached, I was struck by the powerful mix of emotions emanating from her, making it difficult for me to breathe. *Whoa.*

I tried to tap into what was there, differentiate the flavors, but my emotional palate could still use refining. Fear was the most dominant feeling I sensed in the air, but that wasn't unusual; it usually overpowered everything else. Once I could work my way through the thickness of fear, I accessed a surprising pocket of disgust. Had she found her boss disgusting? Had he done something toward the end that she found repugnant? Did she find Stu disgusting for some odd reason?

I didn't have nearly enough information about her or her relationship with Orville to speculate, so instead, I tried to fortify my interior awareness against the exterior emotions, as Nora had been training me to do. I started by focusing on the physical reality around me. I rubbed my thumb and pointer finger together, bringing my mind to the contact between them, focused on my breath moving in and out of my chest, felt the firmness of my feet on the carpeted hallway. Slowly, the assistant's emotions became less stifling.

"Miss Wildes, this is Miss Lilac Heart. Orville's assistant. She, uh... I just informed her of her boss's passing."

I winced empathetically at Stu. "May I speak with her?"

He looked more than relieved to give us space. "I'll just be in the room with Ted. Knock if you need anything."

Once it was just the two of us in the hallway, I turned to the other witch and said, "Lilac?"

My hope was that she would show some sort of recognition that a new person had arrived, but that didn't happen. The only thing that changed about her demeanor was that she went from leaning against the gold-flecked wallpaper to sliding down onto the carpeted floor. Her crying didn't let up an inch.

I chewed on my lip, trying to figure out the best move. She was an important person to speak with in this situation, my Insight told me that much, but I wasn't sure how to approach her. Push too hard, and she might take a dislike to me. Start by comforting her, and we might be here all night. Who even knew if there *was* a way to calm her down from this state?

I was exhausted from the day, and my own basic needs kept me from the degree of patience that might be needed for attempting that. I normally didn't mind people crying around me—it wasn't like I couldn't tell when they were sad anyway, so might as well let it out— but even I had my limits, and this was a lot.

I sat on the floor next to her, providing her some space but not so much that she wouldn't notice me there, and waited to see if the sobbing would run its course.

After a few minutes, it became clear that her emotionality was in a self-perpetuating state. I'd seen toddlers get into this mode before, where they didn't even know why they were crying anymore, but they were caught in a loop. She was young, so perhaps she didn't have a whole lot of practice with self-soothing?

That was the most generous assumption I could give her, as I felt my tiredness settle into my bones. "Lilac?" I ventured again.

"What am I going to doooooo?" She erupted into even louder crying, causing a leprechaun down the hallway to open their door, stick his head out, and shush her.

"I'm not paying top coin to be kept up all night by this yowling!" he barked. "Knock it off!"

Lilac did no such thing, but I did notice an open door to her left, and when I stepped cautiously inside, it only took a very little bit of snooping to find the welcome note from hospitality with her name on it. I returned to the hallway, helped her to her feet, and guided her into her room. She still didn't seem to register that I was there.

As she continued to sob, I slipped her boots off her and guided her into bed. What else was there to do?

Part of me knew I ought to stay with her—leaving someone in this state wasn't the wisest or kindest thing—but, unfortunately, as I set her boots at the end of her bed, I caught a mental glimpse of my bed in my mind's eye, and after that, the idea of staying here to calm an inconsolable stranger for an indeterminate amount of time stopped feeling like a sensible option. I still had one more stop I felt like I needed to make before I could head home and crash out like my entire physiology was screaming for me to do.

"I'll be back tomorrow," I told her, though I was pretty sure she didn't hear me. "We'll speak more then. Just... stay in town, please."

I backed out of the hotel room and closed the door, though I couldn't lock it without the key. She would be fine. Probably. The deputy was in the room across the hall, so it didn't get much safer than that, right? I knocked lightly on the door and informed Stu that I'd put Lilac to bed and would check back the following day. He hollered thank you, but the door stayed closed. I was fine with that. My brain didn't need to cap off the day with a possible murder scene.

When I returned to the lobby, Grim and Monster were wrestling by the couches while Atlas watched from a safe distance.

"You're all still here?" I said. "Figured you'd go back to the house now that you got those treats from the tearoom."

Atlas perked up. *"I'm not leaving you behind."*

As he lumbered to his feet, I scratched him behind the ears. "I appreciate that."

Grim added, *"And we thought you might be heading to somewhere else with food after this."*

"Sorry to disappoint, but I'm heading back to the pottery studio."

Grim's tail dropped. *"Bor-ing! Come on, Monster, let's get outta here. I saw Nora hide some jerky above the cabinets, as if I wouldn't be able to sniff it out. I bet you could reach it."*

Chapter Ten

By the time Atlas and I arrived at Time to Kiln, all the shop lights were off, the closed sign was up, and the door was locked. That was what I figured I'd find.

It was just past nine in the evening, and after such a long and eventful day—and perhaps not a successful one by Raven and Jude's standards—it was unlikely they were still working. There was always the chance that they were still disassembling the tents and such from the week's event, but all of the temporary structures had already been broken down and carried off by the time I arrived.

Oh right. Raven was a South Wind. She had a wand and knew how to use it. That sure made cleaning up much easier. If I'd had a wand and the powers to use it back in New Orleans, I could've made a fortune cleaning houses. I'd been lucky if I could finish three a day, but with magic? I could've *cleaned up*, pun intended. Ten, twelve houses a day...

I was treating myself to that ridiculous fantasy as Atlas and I walked around the side of the studio to the back, where Jude and Raven shared a small house. They weren't married or romantically involved at all. They were simply best friends who'd chosen to build a life together by cohabitating and running a business. I thought the idea was lovely. No reason to be alone just because you hadn't found a romantic partner. Or in the case of Jude, you didn't want one.

"Maybe I shouldn't disturb them," I whispered to Atlas as we reached their doorstep beneath the dim front porch light.

"Don't you think they'd want to know what's happened?"

True enough. "But right before bed?"

"You think they're sleeping soundly tonight?"

Another good point.

I felt so terrible for them. This event that they'd invested so much in had turned into a boondoggle in the final stretch.

I knocked. If they didn't want to talk to anyone, they could simply refuse to come to the door. I wouldn't take it personally.

Jude greeted me a few moments later with a sad smile. His petite frame was backlit by a warm glow from inside. "Dahlia. I'm glad to see you're okay. We were worried about you when you disappeared. Were you overwhelmed?"

I nodded. "I was, but I'm fine now."

So tired I could drop over, but otherwise fine.

"Hello, Atlas," said Jude before stepping to the side. "Come on in, both of you. Raven was just about to pull a peach crumble from the oven. No way we could eat all of it ourselves. Nor should we."

Looked like Grim had made the wrong choice. "A peach crumble?"

Jude shrugged. "She's an emotional baker. It's been..."—he sighed—"a day."

Yikes. I was about to make it even *more* of a day for them.

Their house did smell amazing. The sweetness of the peaches wafted above the toasty scent of the crumble. I worried it would take a gargantuan act of self-control for me to not act like Grim and gobble the whole thing up when no one was looking. However, once Jude led us into the kitchen and I saw just how gigantic of a dish Raven had made, I stopped worrying about that possibility. I'd fall asleep in my chair before managing to stuff all that down.

Wow, though, she really *had* had a day. She'd made enough peach crumble to feed half the town.

"Dahlia," Raven said, waving her wand to gather the last crumbs from the countertops and send them into the compost bin, "we were worried about you."

I stuck my hands in my pockets. "I was worried about you two."

"Oh, don't worry about us," she said. "For my part, I've been through much worse. What brings you by?"

Much worse, I thought.

I decided not to launch right into it. Better that we all got some peach crumble in us before getting to brass tacks. "How did the rest of the competition go? I had to leave. The emotions were—"

"Of course," said Raven. She flicked her wand and sent the last of the dishes into soapy water in the sink, then sighed, tucked her wand into her robe pockets, and braced her hands on her hips. "There wasn't a rest of the competition. It was canceled. Unfortunately, one of our judges fled, and we've been unable to contact him by owl or in person since."

"Orville," I said.

"Correct. Malavic had no problem hanging around. He was more than happy to bask in the chaos." She rolled her eyes. "Let's have some crumble."

Once we were seated around their modest wooden dining table, three mismatched handmade bowls full of the warm, delicious dessert steaming in front of us, Raven asked, "What really brought you by? I know you were worried about us, but that could've waited till the morning."

I looked down at Atlas (his crumble was on a plate on the floor in front of him, and he was under strict instructions to give it a moment to cool before wolfing it down). *"I don't want to tell them,"* I said.

"You don't have to. You have the choice not to."

"But it'll be awkward if I don't," I replied telepathically. *"And they deserve to know."*

"I didn't say it was the right choice. It's just a choice."

I steadied myself, then said, "Orville Ironhelm is dead."

Jude had a forkful of baked peaches on the way to his mouth as I spoke, and he froze with the dessert in midair, his mouth hanging open.

"You're kidding," said Raven.

"I wish I were. His ghost visited me earlier. He died in his hotel room."

Jude set down his fork. "Was he murdered?"

"Nobody knows yet. Deputy Manchester is waiting until the magical examiner and medical examiner take a look at the body before he draws any conclusions. The scene didn't have any obvious signs of foul play."

"That's not uncommon for a murder scene in a town full of witches," said Jude. "They can do it and make it look like nothing. Not so in a place that's mostly weres, I'll tell you that." He shivered. "We like to make it bloody."

Raven frowned down at her crumble like she was going to be sick, and indeed, I felt a wave of nausea hit me that wasn't my own. "It doesn't matter how it happened," she said. "What a mess. What a *mess!*" She put her head in her hands. "You don't even want to know how much we paid for him to be here. We invested so much money in this competition, hoping we would earn back and cover some of the debt from the studio. And now... we're only in more debt. And to the last person we want to be indebted to."

I hated to pry on something as personal as finances, but prying was sort of the whole game when it came to investigation. "Someone lent you the money to pay Orville's fee?"

Raven shoved a full fork of the crumble into her mouth. I wondered if she could even taste it just then.

Jude was the one to answer. "Count Malavic. He heard about the competition and suggested we hire someone like Orville Ironhelm to draw in a crowd. I told him we didn't have that kind of money, and he said he'd be happy to lend it to us, if we decided to go that direction. He was sure it would draw enough of a crowd to cover the loan plus what we needed on top of it."

"So much for that," said Raven around her mouthful.

Malavic. Darn that vampire! He was making it more and more difficult to believe he had nothing to do with Orville's death. Not that I would try to defend him, but I didn't want to have to speak with him if I could avoid it. He was nice enough, but he was also a vampire, and if he was a vampire who might've murdered someone, I could really do without any proximity to him. But it was looking like our conversation would be inevitable now.

His name was like a shark swimming circles around the whole situation.

First, he owned the hotel where Orville died, a hotel he'd bought from something called the Ironhelm Trust.

Now he was the financial backer to get Orville to Eastwind in the first place.

What was going on here? Why did his name keep coming up? Was it a murder plot or something else entirely?

"And now," said Jude, "if we can't pay him back the loan..." Their eyes met, and bitter regret filled the room.

"What was the agreement?" I asked, hoping it wasn't as bad as they were letting on.

Jude was the one to answer while Raven shoved another massive forkful of crumble in her mouth. "If we miss payments to him, he becomes majority owner of the studio."

"Oh no." This was bad. I didn't have to think through all the implications for the Time to Kiln community to know that. "Jude. Raven. I— I don't know what to say. We'll have to ensure you can make the payments, that's all there is to it. Whatever it takes, count me in. You two started this studio, and you did all the work to get it to where it is today. You deserve to make the decision on how it's run."

"He'll still let us run it," Jude said. "He was very clear about that. But he'll get fifty-one percent of the profits."

Raven scoffed. "Joke's on him. That'll be just a

couple coppers each month. Maybe a silver coin if we have a sale or event that brings in more. Hardly even a drop in the cauldron for someone as wealthy as he is."

"Why does he want to own it, then?" I asked.

"I don't think he necessarily does," said Jude, ever the generous one. "He thought we'd make a profit on the competition and be able to pay him back with interest."

Did he, though? I thought, and then wondered when I'd become so cynical.

"He seems to be acquiring more and more properties around Eastwind," I said.

Raven sighed resignedly. "Yeah, that's what they do."

"What's what *who* do?" I asked.

"Wealth hoarders like Malavic. You know he has a massive cave filled with gold, right? Even has his own dragon, Maggie, to guard it all. Why would anyone need all of that? You could buy the whole town a hundred times over with that sort of wealth. Or just hand it out to everyone, and no one would have to worry about money ever again. People in his position get bored, and that goes double for immortals. So they come up with games for themselves to keep things interesting. My guess is his new game is trying to buy up the whole town. Charge everyone rent for everything, keep the money rolling in for him and keep everyone struggling financially."

"Hmm," I said, "I don't think I could ever be bored enough to want to play a game like that."

Raven waved me off. "You also have a conscience, so you'll never be that rich. Malavic doesn't have one of those to hold him back. You give up your soul when you're turned into a vampire."

"Now, now," said Jude, "don't be creaturist. You know the ugly things people say about werewolves. And only *some* of them are true." He shifted his hands into paws and growled. They both erupted in laughter.

It lightened the mood, and that was a welcome relief. I didn't want to think about Malavic any more before I had to fall asleep. The more I heard about him, the less I could imagine that he was just a normal townsperson who also happened to be undead.

I took my first bite of the peach crumble and was transported to another realm completely. Without meaning to, I moaned, causing Raven to grin.

"My mother's recipe," she said. "She was a West Wind. They usually have the best recipes. My only job is to follow her instructions to the letter. If the bake turns out poor, it's always my error."

"Tastes like you had no errors on this one, then," I said, shoving another forkful into my mouth.

Jude poured me a cup of water from one of their never-ending water pitchers—a top seller in the shop— and as I took a long drink, Raven said, "Have you spoken with Dante yet?"

I nearly choked on the water. "About what?"

Raven rolled her eyes, and Jude sighed heavily. "About his saying he loved you. I had the impression that it was the first time he'd said it."

I looked between the two of them for any way out of

answering, but they were locked on to me. Perhaps after asking them such personal questions about their business, it was only fair that I answer this simple one. "That was the first time I heard him say it, yes."

"And have you spoken to him about it yet?" she pressed.

"No. I've been busy. Orville's death and all."

Jude chimed in. "You said his ghost found you at dinner. You left the tent hours before that."

"Good point," said Raven. "He's probably wondering if he's scared you off. Don't you think you should reach out to him?"

"To be fair, he hasn't reached out to me, either."

"Is that his responsibility?" Raven asked. "If he said he loves you and you ran away, it wouldn't be entirely unreasonable to assume you were freaked out by what he'd said and that you needed some space. We've known Dante a long time. He can be forceful when needed, like stepping up to grab the vase from Orville, but it's not his only tool. He can pull back, as well, give people space. I would guess that's what he's doing here."

"I'm no expert on romance," said Jude, "but I do know people. I'd bet he feels like he came on too strong with that forced confession. Maybe even feels ashamed of putting you in that position in public before you were ready to say it back."

"We don't know she's *not* ready to say it back," said Raven, then they both looked at me.

"I... don't know if I'm ready. I've never said it to anybody."

"But you love him," said Raven. "We're not blind. We see the two of you together at the studio. He didn't have to say the words for us to know how he felt about you. You don't have to say the words, either. You love him. It's clear enough."

"Why do people keep saying that?" I snapped.

Raven was unfazed. "Probably because it's true."

"I don't know." I nudged a peach around the bowl with my fork. "I need time to think."

"Promise you'll at least send him an owl before bed," said Jude. "Just let him know you're tired but you want to see him in the morning." When I hesitated, he added, "It's the caring thing to do, and you're a caring person, Dahlia. If we didn't hold you to that standard, what kind of friends would we be?"

"Okay, fine," I said. "You're right. I'll send him an owl when we get home." They appeared satisfied with that, and once our goodbyes had been completed, Atlas and I left the coziness of their small home and stepped outside into a pleasantly breezy late-spring night.

"It's a lot to think about," said Atlas.

"No kidding."

We made for the small footpath around the side of the studio, toward the main road, but as we approached the kilns in the back, something small and furry leaped out from behind one, causing Atlas to yelp and jump behind me.

"It's just Givens," I said, once my eyes adjusted.

Givens was the studio cat. He was a recent member of the Time to Kiln family after his witch—a woman with a corrupted heart—had been sent to Ironhelm Penitentiary for murder.

As her familiar, a part of Givens had wanted to stay by her side, even in those hostile conditions, but she'd cast him off and sent him to live on his own, something most familiars struggled to do after living easy lives of domestication. There was the additional struggle of heartbreak from losing one's witch, too, even in the case of an abused familiar like Givens.

The good news was that he'd taken nicely to the life of a studio cat. I was the only witch outside of Ironhelm Penitentiary who could speak with him, and so I was able to enjoy his transformation. He could communicate with other familiars, who could relay the messages to their witches, but Givens had warmed up quickly to me, since it was a fast way to get his needs met. He told me he was hungry, and I'd lay down a can of tuna for him. No intermediary needed.

He wasn't looking for tuna at that moment, though. Instead, he stalked back and forth across the footpath, his gray tail swaying lazily from side to side. *"I'm not surprised he's dead."*

Atlas and I looked at each other. "Were you eavesdropping?" I asked.

"Of course. What else is there to do? Hunting mice

isn't the never-ending entertainment some cats make it out to be."

"I'll take your word on that," I said. "Why aren't you surprised Orville is dead?"

Givens jumped gracefully onto an overturned clay-reclaiming bucket. *"Because he was arguing with someone back here yesterday. Just behind the kilns. A heated argument. I was hoping it would go to blows, but it didn't. I wouldn't have bet on the goblin, though. Not considering whom he was arguing with."*

I was almost afraid to ask. "Who was he arguing with, Givens?"

His tail flicked back and forth excitedly. *"Don't you want to guess?"*

"Not particularly."

"Fine. You're no fun. It was the vampire."

I groaned. "Not Malavic."

"Yes, Malavic."

"And what were they arguing about?"

Givens jumped off the bucket, padded up to Atlas, and rubbed himself against the hellhound's shaggy front legs. *"I didn't really understand it,"* said the cat.

"Was it money?"

"No. You know that place they sent my witch?"

I nodded.

"The vampire mentioned that place."

"Ironhelm Penitentiary?"

"Yes."

"And he wasn't just saying the name Ironhelm? Because that was Orville's last name."

"*No, he talked about the place. Something about trust.*"

"Trust," I said, "or *a* trust?"

Givens wove between Atlas's back legs and batted briefly at the hellhound's tail. "*What's the difference?*"

"A trust is... Well, I'm not really sure. It's a thing wealthy people have. I wouldn't know anything about it, as a lifelong poor person."

"*Neither would I, as a lifelong cat.*" He hissed, causing Atlas to spin around quickly to keep an eye on him. "*I never liked the vampire. He came around the inn sometimes, too. He smells like death, but not the kind you want to rub your face in.*"

"Right."

"*I know what he's saying,*" said Atlas. "*He's right. You wouldn't want to roll in that vampire.*"

I'd have to trust the familiars on the distinction of what forms of death were and were not appropriate for rolling in. "Anything else you remember from the argument?" I asked.

"*Just that the goblin cursed at Malavic.*"

"Did they leave on good terms, or did they part in anger?"

"*Depends on what you think someone is feeling when they tell someone 'over my dead body.' Is that something people say in anger?*"

"Who said that?"

"The goblin. He told the vampire he could have what he was asking for 'over my dead body.' That's part of why I said I wasn't surprised he was dead. He was talking about being a dead body just yesterday."

That *was* an interesting development.

Frankly, I could go the rest of the night without another interesting development finding me.

It was looking more and more like Orville might've been murdered. And the prime suspect was the last person in Eastwind I wanted to confront.

Chapter Eleven

A guilty conscience kept me from sleeping well that night. It had been late by the time I wrote the note to Dante and sent it off. While he was a night owl from working the dinner shifts at Franco's Pizza so frequently, I didn't necessarily *expect* a response from him before I fell asleep.

Would've been nice, if only to make me feel better about procrastinating so long to reach out, but I wasn't expecting it.

Still, when I woke up the next morning, checked the postbox on the front step of the house, and found nothing inside, I began to worry.

Had my procrastination damaged something between us that couldn't be repaired?

The thought sent a jolt of anxiety through my stomach. I didn't want to lose Dante! I couldn't stand the thought of his moving on from me, dating some smarter, friendlier, more decisive person in town, and my having to see them happy together for the rest of my life.

No, I had to fix this. I loved him. Maybe not in the "I love you" way yet, whatever that actually was, but I cared about him and liked my time with him much more than any time without him. I liked myself better when I was around him, too. Gosh darn it, I wanted to be with him!

While my nerves the night before, when I'd sent off the letter, were mostly around the question of what he would say when he responded, not getting a response at all made me even more anxious. Not the way I wanted to start off the day, but at least it got my blood pumping after a restless sleep.

Who needed coffee when you could start your day with dread?

But no, I still needed coffee. Conveniently enough, I was supposed to meet Margot Penumbra at Necro Coffee this morning. *She*, at least, had responded right away last night when I sent her the letter asking if we could meet. I hadn't told her Orville was dead, but I was curious if word was already starting to spread around town and that was why she'd been so eager to meet. And up so late at night.

Perhaps the whole town was sleepless after what happened at the pottery competition.

The weather was mild, in what felt like the low seventies, with a cloudless sky overhead as Atlas and I made our way over to Necro Coffee. Grim and Monster had opted to head down to Medium Rare for their usual breakfast of scraps, and it was a sign of Atlas's devotion to me that he hadn't gone with them but instead was accompanying me to the café, where the food options were much less greasy and the people who worked there were much less likely to slip him some extra goodies.

Margot wasn't there when we arrived, even though we were a few minutes past the set meeting time. I ordered a coffee and a delicate pear pastry for me and two sausage and cheese rolls for Atlas before making our way to a small table for two.

Necro Coffee, with its large sign on the front window reading, *Coffee so good, it'll raise the dead,* wasn't my first pick of places to meet. That had less to do with the fact that I was a necromancer and the name of the place could be seen as offensive, and more to do with the coffee being good but not great. I'd heard it was better years ago, but there'd been some kind of change in management, and the new folks didn't put as much effort into the experience.

Also, it was overpriced.

I made okay money working at the pottery shop—enough to feed myself and Atlas and pay Nora and Tanner a little bit of rent—but it wasn't anything to brag about, and definitely not enough to make Necro Coffee a regular part of my daily routine.

Atlas had already scarfed down his breakfast when Margot walked through the door, looked around until she found me, then jabbed a finger toward the counter. I nodded, understanding, and she went to order herself something.

"This could be important," I said, already feeling more myself after a pastry and half of my black coffee. *"She had a reason to be angry with Orville after he confessed to thinking her vase was the best but that he wouldn't vote for it to win."*

"Could she have accessed his hotel room yesterday?"

"Hmm... I didn't think to ask Ferin how many people came and went around that time and if he recognized any."

"He might not have told you if you'd asked. Guest privacy, and all."

"Still, I wish I'd thought of it." I tried not to be down on myself about it. I was still new to investigating, after all. *"I'd like to learn more about that clarity glaze."*

"If that's really what it was. Something seemed off about it," said Atlas.

No kidding.

Margot had put some time into her hair and outfit this morning, but the dark circles under her eyes weren't fooling anybody. It looked like she'd slept as poorly as I had last night. Only, she looked miles better because I hadn't even tried with my hair, and I'd merely slipped on a somewhat wrinkled blue blouse and incredibly wrinkled burgundy cotton pants that clashed more than complemented the top. Both had been pulled straight from the worn-once-but-not-dirty clothes pile I'd been accumulating on the chair in my bedroom. Thankfully, the pile could never get too big, because I didn't have that many clothes to my name.

After we said our initial hellos, she cupped her mug between her palms and said, "I'm not in trouble, am I?"

"For what?"

"For the glaze. It didn't turn out how I'd expected. That was probably obvious to everyone there. But it... sort of ruined the entire competition, didn't it? I expect loads of people are furious with me—Raven, Jude, the other contestants, even Orville for how it caused him to confess to all those shady dealings."

I felt my stomach clench. She didn't know about Orville yet. Or if she did, she was doing a good job of playing innocent.

"I don't think you're in trouble with the law, if that's what you mean."

She sighed. "That's something, I guess. And I hope I didn't cause any trouble in your relationship with Dante. I hate that he got wrapped up in the mess. Such a good man."

"No," I said. "Everything's fine there." I was glad I didn't have to hold her vase in that moment, because everything was far from fine in my relationship.

"It was a simple mistake," Margot continued, "but sometimes even mistakes can get you in trouble with the law. My neighbor once blew up her cauldron by adding cilantro instead of parsley to a simple weight-loss potion, and she was fined by the High Council for the danger she caused her neighbors. I don't have the money for a fine."

I made a mental note not to confuse those two herbs in the future, as I wasn't sure I could spot the difference if I'd had a wand pointed straight at my chest. "I spoke with Deputy Manchester yesterday, and I don't think he's particularly concerned with a glaze gone awry. It was intended to be a clarity glaze, right?"

"Wait, you spoke with the deputy? Why? Are *you* in trouble?"

"No."

"Then why did you speak with him? Run into him at the diner?"

I was tempted to say yes, just so we didn't have to get to this point of the conversation so soon, but the truth was better. "I met with him at Cair Crestfall. Orville Ironhelm was staying there. He's dead."

Her eyes went wide. "Wait. Orville or Manchester? Who's dead?"

"Orville."

"Cauldron's curse," she muttered. "Was he murdered?"

"We don't know. But, well, after what happened with his confession..."

She gasped. "You think touching my wonky glaze led to his death in some way?" She brought her hand to her throat, blinking. "Did I kill Orville Ironhelm? Oh goddess, no. Please say that isn't the case."

I could tell she didn't actually mean she wasn't sure

if she'd snuck into his room and murdered him. She was worried her mistake had indirectly led to his death, which was what I thought was more probable myself.

"It could've been natural causes," I assured her. "We don't know anything yet. Deputy Manchester told me he'd let me know when he'd heard back from the magical examiner and medical examiner, but the scene itself didn't indicate foul play."

"It's strange timing, though, you have to admit." She frowned at the surface of her latte. "Goddess, I hope it doesn't turn out that my glaze was involved somehow."

"I hate to even ask," I said, "but could anything in it have been toxic?"

She perked up. "Toxic? Oh goddess, am I a mass murderer?"

"No, no."

Then again, I hadn't heard back from Dante yet.

"*Don't go there*," said Atlas. "*Trust me. I'm a pro at going there. Someone would've told you.*"

I scratched him behind the ears, grateful for the guidance.

"Was there anything in the glaze mix that could, I don't know, be unhealthy, specifically for a goblin?" I asked. "Not to say it killed him, of course."

Margot sighed. "No, I get it. You have to ask. You're working with Deputy Manchester, right? In that free-lance way Fifth Winds do?"

I nodded. "I'm not getting paid, though."

"You really should."

"I do this because it's the right thing to do."

She arched a brow at me. "You think the only people who should get paid for their labor are the ones doing the *wrong* thing?" She waved off her own rhetorical question. "None of the ingredients of the glaze were toxic." She looked away briefly, clutching her drink, then added, "At least, I don't think so. Oh, Dahlia, this is going to sound so bad, but I ought to tell *somebody*. Maybe you can tell me if this sounds like anything, and if not, we can just keep it between ourselves."

I held my breath, not wanting to say the wrong thing and deter her.

She sighed and leaned forward. "After the first day of the competition, once the pieces were in the bisque firing, I was walking home." She kept her voice down. The café was busy with morning business, so I had to really focus to hear her. "Someone started following me. I knew it before I even turned around. I don't know that I heard her so much as felt her presence."

"Whose presence?" I asked.

"I don't know. I wish I did. She was wearing a cloak that concealed her face, and I didn't recognize her voice. It was deep, but it sounded... put on, like maybe she was trying to disguise that from me, too. I don't know. Frankly, I was so disoriented by being followed that I wasn't able to absorb much of those details. She asked me what glaze I was planning on using the following day, and I told her."

"You think she might've tampered with the glaze?"

"No," said Margot, sounding tense. "She didn't tamper with anything. But she did offer me something. When I told her I was mixing up a clarity glaze once I got home that evening, she pulled out a small leather pouch and held it out to me. She said the powder that was inside would be an excellent replacement for the bone ash that goes in a clarity glaze."

"And you trusted her?" I asked.

"Not particularly, but I'd seen what the other potters had thrown and trimmed that day, and I knew if I wanted to get the edge on them, I needed something special. It was worth the risk. She sounded like she knew what she was talking about, too."

I tried to tune into Margot's emotions. Deception wasn't an emotion, unfortunately, but guilt was, and I definitely sensed some of that on her. "Did you ask this cloaked woman why she wanted to help you?"

"Of course. She said she thought I was the strongest potter and she wanted to make sure I won." She paused and chuckled dryly. "My ego bought it, I'm embarrassed to say. So I took the powder from her. She didn't ask for money or anything in return, which should've alarmed me but didn't. Then she left, and I went and added it into my glaze. I think that's what caused the confessions, whatever was in that powder."

"Do you have any of it left?" I asked.

"No, I threw out whatever I didn't use. I... I didn't want anyone to know about it. It felt like cheating. I don't think it was against any of the stated rules, but it still felt like cheating. I shouldn't have done it, Dahlia. You wouldn't have done it if it'd been you, I know that."

"I don't know what I would've done," I said. That was only partly true. I probably wouldn't have trusted a random cloaked stranger to give me the right ingredient, but then again, I wasn't particularly competitive, so I couldn't understand what it felt like to want to win that badly.

"Regardless, it was foolish of me," she said. "You can judge that by the result. Whatever that glaze was, however beautiful it looked, it wasn't a clarity glaze. It was something else."

"You think so?"

"Definitely. Experiencing clarity doesn't necessarily mean you confess to things. I've been trying to think of how to describe it since it happened, and it was like... a compelled honesty glaze or something."

"Is there any chance that it was the opposite? Maybe it caused those who touched it to *lie*?"

She paused. "Huh. I didn't think about that. No, I don't think so. You think Raven lied about the money she spent on bringing Orville to Eastwind?"

Right. I hadn't put that together, but she'd corroborated her own confession when I visited her house the night before. What she'd said when touching the vase and what she'd said when not touching the vase were the same, and I had no reason to believe she was lying to me at her house. There was something unfathomable about telling lies while eating such a delicious peach crumble. It seemed an impossibility.

More importantly, I hadn't sensed any signs of her lying, and since she and Jude had always been open and honest with me in the past, that was likely my best indicator of whether I should believe them or not. They'd earned my trust.

But that did sort of rule out the possibility that the glaze caused people to lie. Which meant Dante…

Ugh, this wasn't like me to be so obsessive over something. I was usually good about putting things straight out of mind, even things that ought to stay in it!

"What did you do after the competition yesterday?" I asked, more to distract myself than anything.

"You mean after I stopped yelling at Danny?" She put her head in her hands. "Oh, Dahlia, I can't believe I acted like that."

"You were upset. It wasn't fair that he'd bribed a judge."

"But to get into a shouting match in public? I'm a grown woman. Liberty said as much, too."

"Liberty Freeman?"

She uncovered her face but slumped in her chair like a chastened schoolchild. "Yes. He declared the competition over and then pulled Danny and me aside. He made us walk all the way up Fluke Mountain to Stews and Brews with him."

I didn't mean to laugh, but I did. "Really?"

"He was right to do it. We couldn't let that animosity

go on. He made us talk it out on the way up there, and then he bought us each a steak dinner. Such a nice man. He didn't have to do it, but he did."

"That was good of him," I said, wishing he'd bought *me* a steak dinner instead of teaching me a lesson by unleashing a shade on the town that nearly destroyed my reputation. "You and Danny Shoehorn were with him the whole time, from when you left the competition through the meal at Stews and Brews?"

Margot nodded. "Yes. It was actually a good thing; I'd skipped lunch because I was nervous about the competition, and I think that might've affected my mood. Oh wait. You're looking for an alibi, aren't you?"

Crinkling my nose in apology, I said, "Yes, sort of."

"Ah! Well, there you go! We went with Liberty Freeman up to Stews and Brews—lots of people saw us there—and we ended up staying for a beer after the meal. Then afterward, we decided to go to Sheehan's Pub for a drink."

"And how long were you there?"

"Too late," she said, chuckling. "I'm a wreck this morning as a result. I hardly ever consume alcohol, so a few drinks over the course of the day..." She shook her head. "When you get to my age, you'll learn that you can either drink alcohol or get a good night's sleep. Not both." She paused. "When was Orville found dead?"

"Much earlier in the evening."

She shrugged a single shoulder. "There you go.

Assuming he didn't die from touching the glaze, then I didn't do it. Danny and I are off the hook."

I'd send an owl over to Liberty Freeman to confirm the alibi, but I was inclined to believe it. Margot didn't strike me as the type to offer such a bold-faced lie that was so easy to disprove.

She struck me as an innocent woman. Innocent of intentional murder, at least. I needed to figure out what the powder was and the identity of the cloaked figure. While there was no proof it was connected to the death of Orville Ironhelm, more and more strange happenings were piling up around this competition and the celebrity judge at the center of it.

As I thanked her for her time, it occurred to me that this was the first interview so far where Malavic's name hadn't come up. Maybe my luck was turning around.

Chapter Twelve

Almost as soon as Atlas and I stepped outside of Necro Coffee, an owl landed on the back of a bench to our left and began hooting at me. I opened my palm to it, and it dropped the parchment from its beak into my hand. I unwrapped the small scrap of paper.

Dahlia,

Sorry for not responding sooner. Late night at work then crashed out as soon as I got home. Darius needed my help on some cabin repairs early this morning, so this is the first chance I've had to respond. I promise I wasn't ignoring you. Wanna get lunch? If so, let's meet at Franco's so we can use my discount.

-Dante

A brick of guilt landed in my stomach. He hadn't been mad or avoiding me. He was just busy doing what Dante did: staying until the work was done and waking up early to help his friends. And all the while, he'd probably been feeling lousy not only about my disappearance, but also the feedback he'd gotten from the judges. I hadn't been there for him on that when he needed it because I was too scared.

You have to stop doing this, Dahlia! You have to be more like Dante and show up for people. You're not invisible anymore. You can't just disappear every time you're uncomfortable.

By the time I'd read the note and finished beating myself up, the owl was gone, so I found the nearest perch, scrawled *see you there at noon* on the back of his original note, and sent it off.

Atlas nibbled my fingers to get my attention. *"Be nice to yourself. You were scared."*

"I'm still ashamed."

"Fear can make us a little selfish sometimes," he said. *"Don't let yourself be afraid of being afraid."*

"When did you become such a sage?" I asked.

"I know a little something about fear. I'm quite the aficionado."

"Oh, Atlas. I wish it weren't so. But I appreciate your advice. I'll try to be nicer to myself."

Even if I didn't feel like I deserved it. Which I didn't.

"I need to find another owl and some parchment to ask Liberty about the alibis. Is it weird that I don't really want to talk to him? That I'm still mad about the shade thing?"

"*No, that whole thing was* way *too scary. We both could've died.*"

I wasn't sure about that, but I didn't bother to correct him.

"Well, you were very courageous throughout it," I said. "You're turning out to be a very brave hellhound."

At that very moment, an owl dropped suddenly out of the sky. Altas jumped and ran to hide behind a bush.

When he peeked his head out, both of us broke into giggles.

* * *

Dante was standing at the bar, chatting with the bartender Trinity, when Atlas and I entered the dining room of Franco's Pizza.

I paused and watched him joke around with his fairy coworker for a moment before he glanced over his shoulder and saw me. His face lit up. Then it tightened. He nodded for me to meet him at an open table on the other side of the room.

He was dressed for a shift, with a white tee tucked into dark brown slacks. He was missing the apron, though, so I assumed he wasn't *actually* on the clock.

"Trinity said she'll bring us over some water," he

said, pulling out a chair for me before taking a seat himself.

We sat facing each other at the four-seater table, and I struggled to look him in the eye. I knew I needed to so that he didn't assume this was a breakup conversation or a rejection of any sort, but it felt impossible to do after I'd failed so supremely as a girlfriend by running away. I was embarrassed and overwhelmed. And a bunch of other emotions I couldn't name.

Funny how I could read other people's emotions, but mine felt like a muddy mess.

"Hey." He leaned forward and offered his hands. Fighting against the invisible resistance of shame, I reached out and grabbed them. "Dahlia, I'm not upset with you."

I forced myself to meet his eyes.

"I'm upset with myself," he continued.

I sat up straight. "What? Why? *You* didn't do anything wrong."

He shook his head. "Listen. When I grabbed that vase, I know you heard what I said. Everyone did." Now I was sure I felt embarrassment, but it wasn't mine.

"It's okay if you didn't mean it, Dante. I'm not even sure what that glaze was."

He squeezed my hands. "I meant it, Dahlia. I'm not embarrassed about that part. What I'm upset about is that I didn't tell you sooner and in private. You're a private person and you would've preferred that. And it's not right that I felt that way about you and didn't say it until some crazy spell coerced it from me. You deserve better than that."

"Oh, Dante, I'm not mad at you for *any* of that. How could I be? You were a victim of the glaze just like all the judges."

"Nuh-uh," he said. "I'm not a victim of anything. Sure, I wasn't expecting it, but I should've been more honest with you, more open. It's definitely something I need to work on."

I almost laughed, shocked to hear he held that opinion of himself. "You're one of the most honest people I've ever met."

"Well, I wasn't honest in this case. Not saying something can be a lie, too. I do love you, Dahlia. I think it's probably obvious to everyone already, but you deserve to hear it. I'm in love with you."

The pause after he finished speaking weighed a thousand tons. It was my turn to say something, and I was pretty sure the thing I was supposed to say was "I love you too."

Too bad my throat chose that moment to stop functioning. There was a constriction in my chest that felt like fear, but why would I be afraid? It didn't make sense, but I was finding it physically impossible to say what he wanted me to say.

"That's fear, all right," said Atlas. *"I can smell it from a mile away."*

Scared or not, I had to say *something.* "Dante, you

know I care about you. I'm not upset with you for saying it. And I do... have love for you."

He shut his eyes and kept them closed, and I felt his grip on my hands loosen. "You... have love for me. How nice. What does that even—" He stopped himself and let go of my hands before leaning back in his chair. "You know what? Don't worry about it, Dahl. I don't need you to feel the same about me. Things don't happen that way. Someone is always ahead of someone else. It's okay." He scooted his chair back. "I actually gotta get to work. Trinity was covering for me, but I'm on the early shift today. Lunch is on me, though. What would you like?"

I tried to speak, tried to say something to respond to the pain and ache I felt coming from him, but all I could manage was, "The chicken parm?"

"And some meatballs for Atlas. On it." He flashed me his best waiter smile and then turned and headed into the kitchen.

"Oh, Atlas," I muttered. "I really botched that."

"*Look on the bright side,*" the hellhound said. "*You still have to interview Malavic, so you may not live through the weekend.*"

"How is *that* the bright side?"

"*At least once you're dead, you don't have to be so scared all the time.*"

Chapter Thirteen

My afternoon shift at Time to Kiln couldn't come soon enough. I'd taken my chicken parm from Franco's to go and nibbled on as much of it as I had a stomach for on my walk over to my job. Customer service was a great thing to lose oneself in. I've heard people complain about it, claiming that some customers don't treat workers like they're fully human, and I think there's some truth to that. But I didn't necessarily mind it. Sometimes it was nice to forget who I was, lose myself in the interaction with the person, helping them find exactly the item they needed from the pottery shop shelves, explaining the details of this bowl or that teapot and speaking to the expertise of the artisan who created it.

In those moments, I didn't have to be me, Dahlia Wildes, a weird witch with a relationship on the rocks and a possible homicide investigation leading directly to the castle steps of the town's vampire.

I'd found two letters waiting for me when I arrived at the shop. The first was from Liberty Freeman confirming Margot Penumbra's story about being with the genie and Danny Shoehorn all day following the botched competition.

The second letter was from Ted, confirming that he'd arrange a meeting with the two of us and Malavic later that night. The plan was to meet at Sheehan's Pub after my shift, and for that reason alone, I wished the shift would never end.

There was so much for me to mentally prepare for ahead of that interview, so many interesting bits from my conversations to string together into coherent questions that might deliver some useful information from the Count, but I didn't have an ounce of desire to do that preparation when the carrot of checking out from myself was being dangled in front of me at work.

I'd regret it later, I was sure. But now wasn't later. Now was now, and now felt just fine as long as I focused on pleasing customers.

That approach was going great until in walked the one person I couldn't possibly pretend was here for shopping. Not when he was in full uniform.

Stu Manchester nodded and muttered hello to a customer who passed him on their way out of the sunlit shop. I looked for a distraction, but the only other people around were a pair of tourists from Avalon who were browsing the tankards but unlikely, based on our previous conversation, to buy anything.

In other words, I didn't have an easy way to avoid speaking with Stu and perpetuating my pleasant break from reality.

Atlas perked up from his spot behind the desk and, to my surprise, sleepily wagged his tail upon spotting the deputy.

"Miss Wildes," said Stu. He looked like he hadn't slept a wink since the last time we spoke, which was likely, considering all the responsibilities he currently carried. "I hate to bother you at work."

"It's fine."

"I wanted to show you this in person." He reached into his breast pocket and pulled out a folded sheet of paper. "The medical examiner's report found the cause of death to be cardiac arrest."

Mostly, I was relieved to hear it. This was a natural death after all, no homicide to be investigated.

But a strange and wild part of me was disappointed.

"Is that what that is?" I said, nodding at the page as he began unfolding it. "The medical examiner's report?"

"No. This is the *magical* examiner's conclusions." He pointed to one of the lines of text. "A high amount of this was found in Mr. Ironhelm's system."

I leaned forward and read the words, but they didn't mean much to me. "Powdered dragon scales?"

Stu nodded. "On a hunch, I brought her the teacup that was found by Orville's body, and she found traces of the powdered dragon scales there, too."

"He ingested it through his tea?"

"Seems like it. I asked her what the substance was used for, and she was as stumped as I was. She said she'd never seen it turn up in any of her magicology reports before, but as far as she knew, it wasn't toxic. You know anything about this stuff?"

I shook my head.

"Thought it might be something associated with necromancy," added Stu.

I shrugged. "If it is, I haven't gotten to that part of the training."

His tired disappointment was evident in the deep lines of his face. I hated to be the source of that.

"I know you have a lot to do," I said. "Orville's death isn't even close to everything on your plate. How about I head over to the Pixie Mixie after my shift ends in a couple of hours and see if Kayleigh and Stella know anything about powdered dragon scales?"

Stu wiped a bead of sweat from his brow. "That's a mighty generous offer of yours, Miss Wildes. A younger version of me would tell you not to worry about it, that I could handle it. But I'm not that young deputy anymore, and all-nighters don't suit me the way they used to. Between you and me, I could fall asleep on my feet right here. So, sure, I would mightily appreciate it if you spoke with the Lytefoots and got back to me about what you find. Just a quick letter via owl would do. Post is completely secure. Anything else I ought to know while I'm here?"

I scrunched up my nose, trying to decide. I gave him

a quick rundown of the people I'd spoken with and what they'd said.

"It all keeps coming back to Count Malavic, doesn't it?" he said.

"Seems so."

"I hate to hear that. He'd not the kind of person I can just go and arrest."

"What about Sheriff Bloom? Could she do it?"

His thick brows crawled up his forehead. "Yeah, I bet she'd enjoy that. We won't get ahead of ourselves, though. Official cause of death is cardiac arrest, and while the dragon scales are a magical anomaly, we don't know that one thing led to the other. Even so, I should have some time to speak with Count Malavic... tomorrow, maybe? Day after? I'm seven reports behind, and I need to fill those out while the details are still fresh in my mind."

"Don't worry about it," I said. "I'm already scheduled to meet with him this evening."

"No kidding? Count Malavic? I hope you're meeting somewhere public."

I was surprised to hear Stu show concern about someone who was essentially a valued member of the town. Apparently, a lot more people harbored discomfort with the vampire than let on. "Sheehan's Pub. And Ted's coming with me."

Stu relaxed visibly. "Ah. Then I won't let it concern me. Ted is a good person to bring along for that. You clearly have your head on straight, Miss Wildes. I look forward to hearing back about everything." He turned to leave but paused before reaching the door. "I'll speak with Sheriff Bloom about getting you a stipend for this work."

"You don't need to," I said quickly.

"No, *you* don't need to. None of the Fifth Winds in this town do. But each of you always does. Don't debate me on this. Miss Wildes. I'm going to get you a stipend. Just, ya know, give me a few days to get to it."

Chapter Fourteen

The bell above the door to the Pixie Mixie twinkled airily as Atlas and I stepped inside the dim apothecary. Light beams through the front window made dust particles sparkle in the air, and Atlas sneezed loudly as I scanned the shop for one of its owners.

I wasn't surprised that Kayleigh Lytefoot was the one I spotted first. She looked very much like a small human (Eastwind didn't have a thing called "human," but it was essentially what every witch looked like), except she had beautiful glossy wings that sparkled as the light hit them just right. She was also gorgeous, with blonde hair that ran down past her shoulders and a soft, un-aging face, despite her being centuries old. Kayleigh was the more sociable of the pixie partners and therefore worked on the customer-facing side of things. Meanwhile, Stella was more of the expert on each of the ingredients and potions they offered and was happy to hide away in the back room, testing products and running experiments. Stella wasn't rude, per se, but she tended to be curt. Nobody around town seemed to mind it, though, because she was so good at what she did.

"Dahlia and Atlas! Good to see you," said Kayleigh, flying over. "I was actually hoping you two would come in soon. Stella's been baking a lot lately, but true to who she is, she's not interested in normal stuff. She's been making treats for familiars, and we need a taste tester."

Atlas's ears perked up.

"Don't worry," said Kayleigh. "Nothing particularly magical about them. Just some calming herbs."

"Why does she want me to let my defenses down?"

I smiled at Kayleigh. "He would love to test one."

She grabbed a small, heart-shaped treat from a glass jar and held it out to him.

At first, I didn't think he'd take it, but then he caught a whiff of it, and I knew he was done for. His nose twitched like mad, and he took a hesitant step toward it. *"This feels like a trap."*

"This is Kayleigh. She has no interest in tricking you."

"Or she's been luring me into a sense of calm this whole time to be able to drug me with a treat."

But then he carefully put his teeth on the treat and took it from her. He only chewed it a few times before swallowing.

She stared down at him. "What does he think?"

"I didn't really get a good taste of it. Maybe I need a second one."

"He approves," I said. "And he'd like another, if that's okay."

Kayleigh laughed, grabbed another from the jar, and offered it up. Atlas didn't hesitate this time.

"Stella will be glad to hear she's onto something." She dusted off her hands and offered me a smile. "What brings you in today?"

Kayleigh was always easy to talk to, and on those occasions where Nora or Ruby sent me to the apothecary to get somewhat shady necromancy ingredients, Kayleigh never batted an eye or gave off any sense of judgment about it. That said, she did keep a close eye on who bought what, and I was glad she did. It'd helped me on my investigations before, even though it was clear she preferred to be discreet about what each customer purchased. Sometimes, however, people were up to no good. I was grateful she didn't seem to ever suspect that of me.

Or maybe she was talented at hiding it.

"I have a quick question for you," I said.

"Of course."

"Do you sell powdered dragon scales?"

Her fluttering wings seemed to speed up, as her mouth tightened almost imperceptibly. "Uh, no, we don't sell those. They aren't legal to buy and sell in Eastwind. On the restricted list and have been for quite some time. There was an incident with their use a while back that left a member of the High Council in disgrace. I think his name was... Oh, I can't remember. Hard to keep the disgraced council members straight sometimes. Anyway, no, we don't sell that item."

I only felt a little embarrassed for asking. Mostly, I found that quite interesting. A banned substance had found its way into Orville's tea before he died of cardiac arrest.

"If someone were to have some powdered dragon scales on hand, what might they use it for?" I asked.

When Kayleigh's brows rose ever so slightly, I felt the need to explain.

"I don't have any, and I don't plan on getting any. But there's been a death, and Stu just got the magical examiner's report back."

"Oh!" she said, clearly concerned. "Who died?"

"Orville Ironhelm."

"Hold on." She closed her eyes and shook her head. "Ironhelm? As in one of the Eastwind Ironhelms?"

"He lived in Avalon, but his family was from here."

"Wow. That's certainly interesting. He's dead from... powdered dragon scales?"

"We don't know that, but it sort of looks that way from the magical examiner's report. The cause of death was ruled cardiac arrest, but there was a large concentration of dragon scales in him, and they found traces of it in the teacup near his body, too. They suspect it might've killed him."

"I don't see how it could," she said.

"Why not? What is the powder used for?"

"It's a truth serum. An extremely powerful one. That's why it's banned. There are potions one can legally brew that lead to honesty and truth, but that's only when the person *chooses* to speak. They can't speak a lie, but they *can* keep their mouth shut. Not so when dragon scales are added to the brew. The powder is a particularly potent form of it, and it *compels* people to tell the truth. It takes away their choice to speak or not speak. Hence the disgraced council person—oh, what was his name?" She wrinkled her nose then shook her head again. "No, still can't remember."

I was much less concerned with the name of some long-forgotten schemer and more occupied with the fact that it sounded like powdered dragon scales might've been the exact thing that the woman in a cloak smuggled to Margot for her glaze. The effects Kayleigh was describing almost perfectly matched what had happened with the judges.

After a heavy sigh, she said, "I think it's the right call to ban the substance. Compelling people to tell the truth, taking away their right to saying nothing, is dangerous and strips them of a basic right to keep their own counsel, to be a private person if they choose."

"Could telling the truth give someone a heart attack?" I asked, not really expecting her to have a definitive answer.

"Anything that stresses a person out enough can

cause cardiac arrest. I've seen people scared to death. Sometimes the truth is terrifying."

"You're right. And Orville Ironhelm didn't exactly strike me as the kind of person who had a lot of experience in telling the truth."

Kayleigh laughed dryly. "That sounds like an Ironhelm. One of the greatest ironies of this town is that the Ironhelms built the prison when they should've all been shut away inside of it."

"Did you know any of them?" It was easy to forget how many townspeople had seen generations come and go.

"I sure did," she said. "They've only been gone from the realm for forty or so years. Not ancient history by any means. I didn't know Orville very well, but his father, Herold Ironhelm, was one of the meanest people I've ever met. He was a jeweler *and* a jailer. Weird combination until you realize that it's all hoarding. Hoarding jewels and hoarding lives. Have you ever been to Ironhelm?"

I shook my head.

"Then you don't know. That place was built from the ground up to destroy hope. People who go in there almost never come out, even if their crime is only minor. An argument could be made that it's for the best, because those who do get out never *really* return to life. Something inside of them is broken by the experience. No matter how much I wish prison were a place where people could be rehabilitated and learn from their mistakes, that's not what Ironhelm is, nor what it was constructed to be. Not even close. Herold Ironhelm exemplified the cruelty of that institution."

"Why did the Ironhelms leave Eastwind? Do you know?"

She shrugged. "To my knowledge, they left because they were about to be put in their own prison. A town can only tolerate so much before they want to fix the problem, and the Ironhelms were quite the problem. All of them were a little weird, but Herold was the worst, by far. I heard he beat someone close to death over a missed payment. Sheriff Bloom was out of patience with them. If I remember correctly, she put Herold in prison once, and he walked right out the next week in a brand-new outfit. The guards were all loyal to him. They wouldn't hold him in there."

"I bet that didn't go over well with the sheriff."

"No. And you don't want to tick off an avenging angel. I suspect that's why they left. Herold might've been cruel, but Bloom has the light of the goddess on her side."

Chills ran down my spine. "I didn't realize she was that powerful. She always seems so nice."

"She's not nice. She's kind. Big difference. Kindness doesn't extend to cruelty, though, just like tolerance can't be extended to intolerance. At the end of the day, if you want the right side to win out, you have to step up to the fight. Gabby Bloom will step up when it's called for."

"If someone were to get their hands on powdered

dragon scales," I said, "and it obviously didn't come from the Pixie Mixie, how would they do that? Import it from Avalon?"

She chewed her lip as she considered that. "There are ways to smuggle things in, sure. Ezra Ares could tell you more about that. But I don't see him wanting to mess around with dragon scales." She tapped a finger to her lips. "There is one other way to get a hold of them in Eastwind."

"And what's that?"

"From the source. From a dragon."

I felt my stomach twist. "Please tell me there is more than one dragon in Eastwind."

She chuckled. "I wish I could, but it's absolutely for the best that we don't have multiple dragons in our realm. They're incredibly territorial. Half the town would burn down if one got a little too close to the other. No, there's only one dragon in town."

"Maggie," I said.

"That's right. Maggie. Count Malavic's dragon."

Chapter Fifteen

Since nearly every conversation led back to Count Malavic, there was a part of me, a brave sliver, that was excited to get to speak with him and ask him questions.

Most of me, however, was freaking out.

As much as my nerves would've appreciated a cold beer, I opted for sparkling water at Sheehan's Pub that evening while I waited for Ted and Malavic to arrive.

Atlas didn't like the pub, partially due to the sticky floors, but mostly because it often became quite crowded and loud. So, even though it was clear he wanted to accompany me out of loyalty, I convinced him to stay home with Monster and Grim.

It was too bad, though, because regardless of how easily frightened my familiar was by most things (he was getting better by the week, but there was still a long way to go), when meeting with a vampire suspected of murder, it was probably better to have a hellhound with you than not to have a hellhound with you.

When the heavy wooden door of the pub next opened and Malavic stepped in, Ted was right there with him. The reaper always carried around his scythe, but he held it casually now, more like a walking stick than a weapon, with the pointy end of the blade sheathed in a thick black leather.

He was off the clock, ready for a relaxing night at the pub of drinks, scufflepuck, and interviewing a possible murder suspect who was also one of his closest friends.

I knew that in Ted's mind, Sebastian Malavic was innocent. Or innocent enough. I doubted I'd be convincing the reaper of anything in our conversation, but perhaps I could at least bring him to the point of curiosity about the clues I'd discovered.

The pub was bustling, mostly with tourists. A local had been murdered in the side alley a few months back, and that had only put a brief pause in the business. The tourists were back and then some now, and they liked to order the kinds of drinks that made Fiona Sheehan roll her eyes the minute she put her back to them behind the bar.

The Avalonians called the establishment "quaint" and "authentic," when they were being generous. They used less-flattering descriptors when their day of sight-seeing and shopping had worn them down. Fiona had a warm heart, but I suspected she could snap on one of the needier customers at a moment's notice.

Sitting in a place like Sheehan's reminded me of walking down the streets in New Orleans. Instead of getting whiffs of strange smells with each block—beignets, sweat, marijuana, sage—I now experienced whiffs of different emotions as people walked by my table and their feelings came and went. It could be overwhelming to be out in public with my powers, as that moment at the end of the pottery competition had more than reminded me, but through some of my training with Nora, I'd learned to ride the waves, so long as they weren't tsunamis. I was getting better at noticing the emotions as they found me instead of completely drowning in them.

"So glad we finally get to speak," said Malavic unenthusiastically as he slid gracefully onto the bench seat across from me. He cradled a glass of red wine in his palm as he looked me up and down.

Ted scooted in next to him, a sweating metal tankard in his hand. He set it on the table, adjusted his robes beneath him, and then leaned his scythe against the wall behind us. I often wondered how he was so casual with that thing, but then again, who would be insane enough to try to steal something from the grim reaper? There was likely magic that protected his tool, as well.

"Ted here has informed me that Orville Ironhelm is dead." Malavic pouted his thin bottom lip mockingly. "Such a sad loss for the scumbag community. What will they do without him?"

I considered asking him if he meant, "What will *we* do without him?" but set that rude thought aside.

"It's true," I said. "He was found dead in his hotel room yesterday. I'm sure Ferin already told you that before Ted mentioned it, right?"

"Ferin?" said Malavic, looking unconcerned.

"Yes, the clerk at Cair Crestfall. You may not have bothered to learn his name, but I'm sure he reported the death to you, considering you're the owner of the establishment."

Ted jerked his hooded face toward Malavic, and I wished I could see his expression in that moment or get a read on what he was feeling. "You own the hotel?"

Malavic took a small sip from his wine, not appearing the least bit frazzled. "I do. A recent investment. To be honest, I'm not terribly involved in the running of it. I prefer not to micromanage. The place was running well before I got it, so I see no reason to interfere and be heavy-handed."

"Hold on," I said. "Did you just hear about Orville's death from Ted, or did Ferin already mention it?" Had I already caught the Count in a lie?

"The clerk notified me of a death on the premises, but that's part of the hospitality industry. When you own hotels and inns, you're going to have people pass away. Sometimes on purpose, but mostly it's just a numbers game. When schedules are disrupted, when people are on vacation and perhaps not getting the sleep they usually require, medical events happen. People can suffer cardiac arrest, say."

It felt like he was toying with me, but I tried not to let that derail me. "Did you know Orville would be staying in your hotel when you offered to finance his trip and judging fee?"

"It's not *my* hotel in the way you mean it. It's a hotel I own and profit from. And if you remember, I also own Malavic Manor Inn. I plan on buying up the Ram's Head Inn soon as well, if those minotaurs ever settle on a price. I would buy those cabins out from under Darius Pine up on Fluke Mountain, too, if I could convince him to take his paws off them. It's just business, Dahlia. I feel no attachment to any of the properties."

"Wait a minute," said Ted. "You paid for Orville to come and judge the competition? I thought you hated the Ironhelms."

Being held accountable by a friend was the closest thing to making Malavic uncomfortable that I'd seen so far. He looked back and forth between Ted and me, his glass of wine forgotten in front of him. "I didn't finance it because of who he was. If they had been trying to get some other judge whose family I *didn't* personally despise, I would've still made Raven and Jude the offer. So, really, I was quite a good person by not letting my grudges keep me from helping my fellow small-business owners."

"Why did you bother to offer them the loan at all?" I asked, though I suspected I already knew the answer.

Malavic seemed to conduct his business more like a mobster than a philanthropist.

He shrugged. "A competition like that? It draws a crowd. Listen, I know your bestie Nora feels a certain way about how I conduct myself, but I'm a businessman. If you think I shouldn't capitalize on the tourism boom in town, then you are anti-business, and that's all there is to it."

"That's what the offer to Raven and Jude was about?" I asked. "You wanted to draw more Avalonians to town for the competition?"

"So they would book rooms in my hotel and inn, yes. More people in town means more people needing a place to stay. You can be upset with me for thinking strategically and making sure to position myself for the moment, but that doesn't mean I had anything to do with Orville's death."

"If you're so set on making money, why did you comp his room?" I arched a brow at him. He clearly didn't realize how much information I'd been gathering over the last couple of days.

But he only laughed. "Why did I comp the room of the judge we were paying to be here? It was part of the compensation package, my dear little death witch. Throw in a few nights at a fancy hotel to sweeten the deal. You don't actually think someone with the clout of Orville Ironhelm would agree to judge the competition only to have to pay for his own hotel or stay in some local's smelly guest house, do you?"

It was a fair point. Since Malavic was financing most of the goblin's fees, he might as well use what resources he had to sweeten the deal. A room for Orville was easy enough.

Dang. Had I been completely offtrack with Malavic?

But no, there was still plenty to talk about while I had him.

"What were you arguing with Orville Ironhelm about behind Time to Kiln on the second day of the competition?"

Malavic's mouth opened, but he didn't speak immediately. "I don't know what you're talking about."

"I spoke with someone who overheard you two arguing. Orville said something about 'Over my dead body.' A day before he turns up dead—you have to admit, that's strange."

While I couldn't see Ted's face, it was clear from his motionless posture that he was locked on to his friend, waiting for an innocent explanation.

"I hated the man," said Malavic. "That's no secret. I hated his family, too. Everyone did, when they were around. But memories fade too quick, even among those who were here when the Ironhelms ran around, causing their usual trouble. I was simply letting Orville know that while he was welcome to judge the competition, he was not welcome to get cozy in this town."

Not sure how much I bought that, I said, "You think he was considering sticking around?"

"I wasn't sure. I wanted to make sure the thought didn't cross his mind."

I wasn't sure where the courage came from inside of me for the next question. Perhaps I was already in so deep that a step further didn't feel any less reckless. "Why mention the Ironhelm Trust, then?"

Malavic stiffened. "I don't remember bringing that up. If I did, it was likely to remind him that just because the trust still owned the penitentiary didn't mean he had any claim to residing in this realm."

"The same trust that owned Cair Crestfall before you bought it, huh?" I asked.

Malavic rolled his eyes. "You're trying to connect dots that don't belong together. Let me tell you a little bit about how business works around Eastwind. Someone or a family with money buys up things. Undoubtedly, they begin to hemorrhage money because they got too greedy or they left the property to some degenerate heir. Their empire begins to disintegrate, and when that happens, someone else with money comes along and buys it up."

"Is that what you're doing now?" asked Ted. "Buying up everything in Eastwind?"

"Not everything," said Malavic, reassuringly. "Just what I can get for cheap. The Ironhelm Trust is weakening, thanks in large part to Orville's poor business sense. He spends—apologies, *spent* money far too quickly. He's been draining the trust for years, and, yes, when an opportunity to take some of the Ironhelm property off their hands arises, I'm happy to step up. Would you rather some rich investor from Avalon come in and buy it? Plenty are interested. They would turn this whole place into a theme park if they could, with every East-winder being an unpaid actor. I'm doing the town a huge favor by outbidding competitors, and on my own dime. This is the only way to keep Eastwind as it is during the influx of interest from Avalon." He took a sip of his wine. "You're welcome."

If what he'd said was true, the town did owe him a debt of gratitude. I'd seen outside investors buy up half of New Orleans after the last big hurricane, turning homes into vacation rentals and forcing the town to subsist on money from tourism more than ever. When people did their best to rebuild their lives after the flooding receded, they were forced to do so at higher prices that many couldn't afford.

But.

But.

That was assuming that what Malavic claimed about Avalonians trying to buy up property in Eastwind was true at all. I had no idea about any of that.

So, rather than thanking him, I decided to poke at another question that had been simmering in my mind. "Did you give Margot Penumbra powdered dragon scales for her glaze?"

Malavic chuckled. "Of course not. I didn't even know who she was until the competition began. Just some local witch. Not very interesting. Her glaze was quite something, though. Powdered dragon scales, you say? Was that an ingredient? Makes sense, with how it turned out. What a show that gave the audience!"

"Powdered dragon scales are dangerous," said Ted. "They compel the truth. I had to guide someone to the other side once as a result of dragon scales. The truth can be deadly." He shook his head mournfully. "People ought to be able to decide what they say, and when."

I turned to Malavic. "I already confirmed that powdered dragon scales aren't sold in Eastwind. You're the only person who owns a dragon."

Malavic yawned, shrugged. "Maggie sheds every few years. It's a necessary process for dragons. I have to do *something* with all those scales so that they don't build up in her cavern. If people misuse a natural substance, you can hardly blame *me*. That's yet another thing the town owes me great thanks for. The service she provides in guarding the treasury is irreplaceable."

I did my best not to roll my eyes. Malavic was really something. Instead, I followed the line of questioning. "Fine. What do you do with the scales that she sheds?"

He waved his hand around. "A little of this, a little of that. I just need them out of her way."

I considered pushing more, but I could tell he wasn't going to budge. There would be no accountability from him on his disposal of those scales.

"After the competition fell apart and Orville's assistant led him out of the fray, where did you go?" I asked.

He raised his hands, gesturing to the room. "Here. It

was all quite entertaining, but it was clear the competition had fallen apart as a result of that glaze. Nothing more was needed from me, as the other contestants were already missing a judge and wouldn't be able to get their final scores... as if that mattered once one of the judges confessed to being bribed. Initially, I stayed right where I was at the judges' table, enjoying the scene. Margot and that elf nearly went to blows, but Liberty ruined it all by interfering. It became dull quickly after that, so I decided to head here for a celebratory drink."

"Celebratory?" I said, hardly believing that was the word he'd use.

"Of course."

"But the competition was a disaster."

"Yes, but again you show how little business acumen you possess. It's clear you've already spoken with Raven and Jude and understand the arrangement we made. When the competition blew up, it was obvious they wouldn't be able to pay me back the money I'd lent them, therefore I'd just acquired the majority ownership of a new business in town. That's something worth celebrating to a businessman."

"You're taking their business out from under them?" said Ted. "Sebastian. That's not very nice. Jude and Raven are good, hardworking people."

Malavic shrugged dismissively. "Don't get into business if you can't handle it, I suppose. Plenty of jobs around town that don't require being a business owner. Besides, have you *seen* those two? They're artisans, teachers, sure, but not businesspeople. They don't want to deal with all the numbers. I'm doing them a favor, really."

I knew Raven and Jude didn't see it that way, but I wasn't here to debate with the vampire.

"You went straight here from the competition?" I asked.

"Didn't even stop by Mancer Academy to drink the blood of children," he said before smugly sipping his wine.

"Can anyone vouch for you coming straight here?" I asked.

Ted raised his hand. "I caught up with him just as he was a street over from the studio. I was heading this way after finishing a particularly tricky crossword at Medium Rare. Heh."

I had no reason to disbelieve Ted. "You're sure he was coming straight from the competition?"

"I'd say so. I heard a big crowd still over there. Figured the thing had just wrapped up and he was heading to the pub before the tourists filled it and there weren't any tables left."

"You didn't talk about what happened?" I asked.

Ted and Malavic looked at each other. "No," said Ted. "We were talking about the new spin I'm learning in scufflepuck. This particular wrist movement." He acted it out for me. "It's good for circumventing the opponent's puck in the last third of the board. I read about it in a book from the library and wanted to practice it."

"And how long did the two of you stay here?" I asked.

"All day," said Ted. "I went straight to the hotel from here when I got the tingle."

"The tingle?" I repeated, trying to follow along.

"The death tingle. It's a little tickle in my chest, then it feels like a magnet. Draws me to the death so I can find the soul."

"Speaking of which," Malavic interrupted, "have you communicated with Orville yet? Seems like all of this could be cleared up if you did."

I felt defensive, like Malavic was telling me how to do my job, even though this was very much volunteer work despite Stu's insistence on getting me a stipend.

Also, I was supposed to be the one asking the questions!

"Orville has dropped in, yes," I said.

Malavic addressed his next question to Ted. "And have you taken him to the other side yet?"

"Nope. He isn't ready."

"Unfinished business?"

"Sort of," I replied. "I think he's worried about the damage that confession did to his reputation."

To my surprise, Malavic threw his head back and laughed. "Oh yes, taking bribes is the thing that will finally tarnish an Ironhelm's reputation." Sarcasm dripped from every word. "Foolish goblin. What a vain and foolish goblin."

"I don't know," I said. "He worked hard to become an excellent potter."

Malavic waved that off. "He only made a few of the works he's credited with, and the least interesting of them at that. He's been using his family's wealth to buy pieces from disadvantaged potters and sell them as his own. He would've gotten to that in his confession, I'm sure, if your hero boyfriend hadn't swooped in and ruined all the fun."

Was that true? Was Orville a fraud through and through? Or was Malavic's grudge showing in the form of ruining what shred of a positive reputation Orville still had left to him?

"Speaking of his confessions," said Malavic, "what do you remember of them?"

"He confessed to bribery. In this competition and previous ones."

"Hm," said the vampire. "No more specifics than that?"

"I'm sure there were specifics," I replied. "But we were all in a bit of shock, weren't we?"

He nodded somberly. "Disappointing. I'd hoped you'd be a better investigator than Nora, but it seems you have a ways to go. And even further before you get close to the skill Ruby True used to have, before she went completely insane."

"Ruby's not insane," I said, bristling.

He smirked. "You should've seen her in her prime. Quite something. Now she faffs around with Ezra Ares, does almost nothing else but read romance novels at home and grow deadly plants in her garden. I don't think that tea helps. The one from A New Leaf. She was already losing her mind, and the mushrooms have accelerated it, clearly."

"I think she's fun," said Ted. "And some of those books she reads are fun, too. She recommends them to me when I run into her at the library. I have a few at my cabin, assuming one of the phoenixes hasn't set the stack on fire yet. Heh."

Malavic didn't comment further on that. "The bribes were an interesting part of his confession, yes. But they were simply a delicious seasoning to the main dish." He motioned for Ted to get up and let him out of the booth. As the vampire stood, he said, "Go ahead and put your drinks on my tab. I'm doing all right for myself, and this conversation has been surprisingly stimulating." He nodded to both of us, and then swooped out of the pub.

Chapter Sixteen

While I'd gathered some useful information from Count Malavic, it wasn't nearly as much as I'd hoped for, and there was still work to be done.

I needed to speak with Orville's assistant. While she was no longer in such distress as the day before, Stu informed me that he'd struck out in his attempt to interview her. In the note he'd sent, he said he suspected she might need a softer touch than he could offer in his current sleep-deprived state, and that I might be more successful, as a younger woman myself.

Orville's assistant, Lilac, had been moved to a different room in the hotel, one farther away from where her boss had been found dead. We didn't arrange to meet in her room, though. Instead, we met downstairs in the tearoom again. Two nights in a row. Good grief. At least I got to enjoy another cup of the lavender tea, even though this time it was going to be on my own dime.

It occurred to me, as I arrived at the hotel, that I hadn't eaten since lunch. Hoping that the stipend Stu had mentioned would actually come through, I ordered a cucumber sandwich with my tea once the pixie server came by our table.

Lilac appeared to be in a better headspace than the last time I'd seen her. She wasn't emitting such an emotional maelstrom. I could still sense heaviness in the air around her, and her eyes were puffy from crying beneath her thick glasses, but she held herself with more dignity, sitting up straight and even offering me a kind smile once the pixie left us and I thanked her for meeting with me again.

"Are you, like, a freelance detective?" she asked.

"No, not quite."

"They have a bunch of those in Avalon. Private investigators, bounty hunters. Not a whole lot of deputies or sheriffs, and none of them are as kind as your deputy here."

"Yes, Deputy Manchester is a great man."

She nodded. "I'm afraid I wasn't very kind back to him. Or very useful. I know he meant well, but the questions he was asking... It's all very fresh still. I'm not used to being so emotional. I pride myself on keeping it together and not making my emotions a problem for anyone else."

I could certainly relate. "Don't worry. I'm sure he didn't take it personally. He's a kind man, but he's still law enforcement, ya know?"

She narrowed her eyes at me. "And you're not?"

"No. I'm just a witch."

"What kind?"

"A Fifth Wind."

Her mouth fell open. "A death witch?"

"I don't... I don't call myself that."

"But you can see spirits and do necromancy, right?"

"Yes."

"Wow." She leaned back in her seat, staring at me like I was some oddity beneath a glass case. "They don't have any of those in Avalon that I know of. I think they ran them all out or killed them." Then she quickly added, "But I'm glad they don't do that in Eastwind!"

"Me too," I said earnestly.

"You help out the sheriff and deputy a lot?" She looked much more comfortable now as she sipped her tea.

"Not really. This is only my fifth time."

"In how many months?"

I counted in my head. "About seven?"

"That seems like a lot. Do people get murdered frequently in Eastwind?"

"You suspect your boss was murdered?"

Lilac's expression tightened, and I felt a small jolt of her fear shoot through me. "I don't know. It seems likely, doesn't it? Why else would you be talking to me about it, right?"

"I'm only gathering information at this point. The main thing I keep running into is that no one in town knows Orville well enough to help us understand the situation. Except you. Tell me about him. What was it like working for him?"

She wadded her napkin in her hands, staring down at it. "It was fine."

The hint of disgust wafting around her begged to differ.

"How long have you been working with him?"

"About as long as you've been working with the deputy. Around seven months."

"And what did you do before that?" I half expected her to say "nothing," as she looked young enough for this to be her first job out of school. But instead, she said, "Odd jobs. Mostly domestic labor for the wealthy. Babysitting, cleaning homes. It's like that in Avalon. If you're not one of the wealthiest people there, you're scraping together what you can to make sure you can afford at least one meal a day."

"I didn't know that about the realm," I said. Leading into this investigation, I'd imagined Avalon as some sort of haven of riches and vitality. My idea of it was rapidly changing, though.

"If you go, you'll see," she said. "It's not like here, where everyone takes care of each other. Nobody checks in on their neighbor over there. At least, nobody ever checked in on me. If I wanted to pay my rent and not starve, I had to figure it out on my own."

I felt a sudden kinship with her. On the one hand, it sounded like her experience in Avalon mirrored mine in

New Orleans. Angelina and Donovan had certainly been keeping an eye on me back there, and I was pretty sure they wouldn't have let me starve, but none of my clients would've shed a tear if I'd starved to death. They probably would've felt put out that they had to find a new housecleaner.

Then I remembered that, technically, I *had* died in New Orleans, though not of starvation, and all of my usual clients had probably felt *very* put out by it.

Oh well.

Meanwhile, when I'd arrived in Eastwind with nothing to my name, I came to a community that made sure I had what I needed. Nora had given me something to eat and a place to stay. Raven and Jude had hired me to work at the shop, even though I didn't have a resumé or any experience in retail. And come to think of it, I hadn't seen a single person begging on the streets of Eastwind. Not one the whole time I'd been there.

People did take care of each other here. It would likely be a culture shock to return to a place like New Orleans, where someone else's misfortune that landed them on the streets was considered an unsightly inconvenience.

I had no idea Avalon was like that, too.

"I don't know what I'm going to do now with Orville gone," said Lilac miserably. "I'll have to start searching for a new job, I guess, but everyone's going to ask about my last one, and I'm going to have to tell them my employer was killed!" She started crying, soft, self-pitying sobs.

"We don't know that he was murdered yet, Lilac. It's possible he simply had a heart attack without there being any foul play." I questioned why she wouldn't accept the possibility of natural causes. Did she know something I didn't, or did the idea of her boss being murdered simply fuel her self-pity best?

"I have no one to go back to," she said. "No reason to go back." She clutched at the charm of a necklace she wore as she blinked up at me. "Maybe I can stay here. Maybe I can let Eastwind take care of me."

"You could," I said. "That's an option."

She swallowed against the tears and rubbed her thumb over the metal in her hand.

"Is that a locket?" I asked.

"What?" She clutched the charm tighter to her chest.

"Your necklace. It's beautiful. Is it a locket? I always wanted one of those, but I never knew whose picture to put in it. Too many siblings, and I wasn't close with my parents. Didn't have a boyfriend, either."

She opened her fist and presented the heart-shaped charm in her palm, leaning closer so I could get a better look. Etched into the front was a crest. A heart with a sword through it. She opened it and showed me the pictures inside. Each was of a young woman who looked strikingly like Lilac and appeared around the same age, and only when I looked more closely could I confirm it was two different women.

"Is one of these your mother?" I asked.

She nodded. "Mother and grandmother. I don't remember them. I was too young when they died. My sister raised me for a while, but then she got married and her husband didn't want me around, so I was on my own."

"How old were you?"

"Twelve."

I gasped. "Lilac, that's so young."

She shrugged and closed the locket, tucking it back into her blouse. "I wish it hadn't happened, but it did. Like most things in my life." I tuned in and felt the sting of bitterness she caried in that heart of hers behind the locket.

While I hadn't felt particularly bitter about my unfortunate childhood and upbringing, I could understand how someone else might. Especially being kicked to the curb at twelve. I shuddered to think about what she might've had to do to survive.

Thankfully, that wasn't the focus of our conversation.

"How did you come to work for Orville?" I asked.

"I saw a listing for the job in the local paper."

"Really?" I couldn't imagine someone like Orville, who was supposedly well connected in Avalon, publishing an ad in the paper for an assistant. Wouldn't he rather take a recommendation from one of his connections? Maybe hire one of their children?

"Yeah, I saw it listed there," she said, "and I applied.

The interview process was rigorous, but eventually I won out. He said he liked my initiative. If there's one thing a person like me needed to survive this long, it's initiative. Hunger is good for inspiring that."

"And how did he treat you?" I asked. "Was he a good boss?"

"He usually paid me on time," she said in a noncommittal way that made it crystal clear she was trying not to speak ill of the dead.

"That doesn't make someone a good boss. That's meeting the bare minimum legal requirement."

She sipped her tea and leaned back in her chair. "He couldn't be a great boss because he wasn't a great person. I'll admit that, even though I know it makes me sound like I might've done something to kill him. I don't think you'll speak with anyone who knew him that would say differently. He was liked by his fans and admirers, sure, but he couldn't keep people in his life. I was the only person who was consistently around him, and only because he paid me and I needed the money. He didn't have any friends. He knew people around Avalon, but he ran in this group of artists that... They aren't very talented, Dahlia. They're rich and bored. That doesn't make you an artist. They haven't experienced enough hardship to be true artists, perhaps." She paused to sip her tea. "Orville only paid me when I reminded him to. And then he made me do it myself."

"Made you do what yourself?"

"Made me do all the accounting. Made me manage

his money and take out exactly what I was owed. I wish I hadn't been so honest about it, but I wanted to keep my job. In retrospect, it probably would've been smart to skim a little extra and save it for a rainy day. It wasn't like I had a fantastic salary with benefits or anything. I could afford rent, some meals, and when we went out to eat together, I would use his money to pay for my food and drink as well. He didn't even notice, he had so much." She pressed her lips into a thin line. "The goblin didn't need the bribes, Dahlia. He had plenty of money, from what I could see. I don't know why he kept taking them."

"Did you know about the bribes prior to the confession at the pottery competition?" I asked.

"I had my suspicions. Like I said, I was in charge of his finances. Every time he would judge a competition or speak, there would be the fees he received that were intended to be listed as basic fees—though they were high enough that I could've lived off a single one for a year—and then there would be additional money that came through. He told me not to keep records of that and simply to hide the coins in the cellar."

"Interesting," I said. "Does anybody else know about the coins in the cellar, now that he's dead?"

"No, which is why I'm such a fool!" She threw her arms into the air. "Why didn't I take some of that for myself? Why did I have to be so *honest*?"

I didn't point out that if no one else knew about the stash, she could very well return to Avalon and take it all for herself. Perhaps she was too honest to realize even that much.

"Did you ever report the bribes?" I asked.

She looked at me like I might've hit my head prior to our conversation. "Report to whom? I never had any proof, only a strong suspicion that something wasn't right. And like I mentioned, your upstanding Deputy Manchester isn't a good reference for what the authorities are like in Avalon."

"So, your sheriff isn't an angel?" I asked. For some reason I'd assumed every realm would have an angel in charge of enforcement, perhaps even an avenging angel like Sheriff Bloom.

Lilac laughed. "Not even close. If I'd reported Orville for bribes, nothing would've happened outside of me losing my job. There aren't great options for honest people in Avalon, Dahlia. You seem like a truthful, hard-working person, so I hope you never find yourself living there. You wouldn't do well."

She was probably right about that. I wasn't rich in Eastwind, if you simply counted up the money I had in my name, but it was rare that I felt that paucity because I had so many friends who were willing to give what little they had whenever I needed it—a meal, a favor, or even just a sympathetic ear. That was a richness no amount of money could buy.

My mind flashed to Count Malavic, perhaps the wealthiest person I knew, and I remembered his parting words at the pub. There was more to the confession than the bribe. What was it?

"What else was Orville up to?" I asked. "Since he's dead and you're out of a job anyway, you might as well let it all out, right?"

Lilac rolled her eyes. "What *wasn't* he up to, really? If there was money in it, he'd give it a try."

"His family owns the penitentiary here, did you know that?"

Her brow furrowed. "He has family here?"

"Well, not anymore, from what I've heard. I'm still trying to get to the bottom of it. But the prison in Eastwind is called Ironhelm Penitentiary, named after his family."

"You sure it's not a coincidence?" she asked. "As far as I know, the Ironhelms were an Avalonian family. Maybe there's, like, a distant cousin who owns the prison here."

"No, he definitely mentioned something about it when he was touching that vase. Oh!" A sliver of a memory popped back in. "He said something about... falsely testifying? No, what was that? He did something to a family to make sure the Ironhelms could buy the prison, but..." I shook my head. "I can't remember it exactly. Did you hear him say anything about that at the competition?"

She scoffed. "I don't remember much of what he said there. I was at the back of the crowd, taking a quick break to eat a sandwich after dealing with his temper all day. I heard him say something about bribes, and that's all my brain absorbed. I ran around the crowd as fast as I could to try to get him out of there."

"You were trying to protect him," I said.

"Of course I was. I can't have him losing every work opportunity available by destroying his reputation. He'd have no need for me, and then I'd be out of a job."

"It had nothing to do with caring about him?" I asked.

She didn't even pause. "No. I don't... I didn't care about him. He was a goblin not even a mother could love. He was all appearance, and even that appearance was a lie. There was nothing beneath the façade, as far as I could tell."

I hated to think that poorly of someone, but from my brief interactions with his spirit, I couldn't dispute her claims.

"One last question," I said, "because I can see you're done with your tea, and it's been a long couple of days for you. Did you have a key to Orville's room?"

"No. The hotel comped us two rooms, so we weren't staying together. Oh gosh, can you imagine?" She shuddered. "I can't. I won't. Not that I have anything against goblins in general, but he was three times my age and..."

"So, no key," I said.

"No. I only had the key to my room. Wait." Her eyes went wide. "*He* didn't have a key to *my* room, did he?"

"Not that I know of," I said, and she seemed to relax. "Both of your rooms were free of charge?"

"Yes. And still are. The owner said I could stay here for a couple of extra days before going home."

"You spoke with him?" I asked.

"No. The clerk relayed the message. The faun."

"Ferin," I said. "He seems nice."

"He seems scared of his boss," she said.

Considering who his boss was, I couldn't blame him.

I thanked Lilac for her time and, knowing she was now unemployed without any clear job prospects, dug into my pockets to cover the bill for both of us. It was what anyone in this town would've done for me, had I been in her position. It was what they *had* done for me.

I wasn't sure if she'd meant it when she said she was considering staying in town, but I hoped for her sake that she did.

Chapter Seventeen

This investigation was dragging on longer than I'd hoped. I woke up the next morning after a series of confusing dreams that involved Malavic dancing in a pile of gold while Lilac begrudgingly tossed coins his direction.

Atlas was still deep asleep, his legs twitching, when I sat up in bed and tried to remember what day it was and whether I was working the morning or afternoon shift at the shop. When I remembered that Sasha had the morning shift covered, I was extremely tempted to sleep in.

But Nora and Tanner would be back later this evening, and I'd hoped to have this thing with Orville wrapped up by the time they arrived, solely to be able to impress them with how I could handle things on my own.

If they thought the town couldn't get on without

them, they would be unlikely to take a vacation again. Nora was one of those hyper-competent people, borderline a superhero, who made everything her responsibility if no one stepped in to stop her from it. I admired her for that, but I also wanted to do my part as her friend to remind her that the world kept turning if she took a break.

So, I dragged my backside out of bed. *Ugh.*

I sent off an owl with a message I'd written out in my head on my walk back the night before, then made some breakfast—oatmeal for me, and bacon and eggs for the familiars. Atlas was my main concern, since he insisted on accompanying me on my stops that morning, so he received the largest portion. But don't worry about Monster and Grim, because not only did they get some scrambled eggs and bacon from me, but they left right after it to go get more scraps from Medium Rare. I cooked Atlas a second helping once they were gone.

By the time I'd finished my breakfast and tea, I'd received a reply from Landon. It was all set, then.

We made our way to the Parchment Catacombs, and a half-hour later, we were deep in the dimly lit tunnels with Landon Hawker.

The North Wind witch had worked in the Parchment Catacombs, where all the records and paperwork of Eastwind were stored, for years, and he knew his way around. It was clear that someone could get lost in there until they died of dehydration, if they didn't have his expertise. When I mentioned that, he informed me that it was by design. Rather than hiring security guards, the folks who first dug the tunnels used disorientation as their security system.

The cavern we found ourselves in was well finished, unlike some of the rooms we'd passed, where the walls were still mostly rough rock, and the floors were compacted dirt. This one had large flagstones for us to step on, and the walls had been finished with heavy wooden beams that arched over us, supporting the ceiling. I hadn't thought about the possibility of a cave-in until I saw those beams.

I wasn't one to be claustrophobic, but it took a certain kind of person to spend all day in a place like this. Landon was that special kind of person, clearly. Grace once explained to me that he became so absorbed in the documents he filed and transcribed that he didn't even realize he was underground most of the time he was at work.

This room had plenty of torches around the walls, so the darkness didn't feel oppressive while I waited for Landon to find what we needed.

His fingertips danced over the edges of pages as he searched through the massive filing cabinet. "There it is." He pulled out a sheet of parchment, held the edges to keep it stiff, then began silently reading.

"Is that it?" I asked.

He didn't seem to hear me.

A new light source appeared suddenly to my right, and both Atlas and I jumped. Landon gave no indication that he'd seen it, but of course he didn't, because he couldn't have seen it even if his nose hadn't been in the document.

Orville Ironhelm's ghost floated next to me, his arms folded, a scowl on his face. "Why aren't you trying to find my killer and clear my name? That was obviously a lying spell in that glaze, and now everyone thinks I'm a fraud and a criminal. Yet here you are, deep underground, wasting the day away."

"It wasn't a lying spell," I said.

Landon looked up. "Huh?"

"Nothing. Talking to the dead guy. You can go back to reading."

He nodded and then did just that.

"Of course it was a lying spell," said Orville. "You don't actually believe I would stoop so low as to accept bribes, do you?"

"I'm starting to," I said, "but only because I keep talking to people who think you would."

"Lies!"

"Margot's glaze didn't make people lie, Orville. It compelled them to tell the truth. Apparently that's illegal, but still. I feel confident that what everyone who touched the vase said was the truth. I've all but verified that."

He turned up his nose. "You clearly haven't, because it was all lies from me."

"I don't think you know the difference between truth

and lies," I said. "You might know the difference less than anyone I've ever met."

"You have no idea what you're talking about!"

"Ah!" said Landon. "Here it is!" When I turned around, the parchment was laid out flat on small table next to an old newspaper. "Come look!" I joined him at the table, where he pointed at the document. "This is the deed for the penitentiary. You can see here"—he pointed to a line of text—"when the deal was finalized. That was fifty-three years ago."

I nodded, trying to follow along.

"This issue of the *Eastwind Watch* was published only a week after the deal was finalized." He pointed to an article with the headline *Ironhelm Testimony Secures Deal, Fate for Rivals*.

"Those were in the same file?" I asked.

"Yep. This is the Ironhelm room."

"The Ironhelms have their own room in the catacombs?"

Orville chimed in. "Of course we do. We're an important lineage in the realm."

Interesting take, considering there were no more of them in Eastwind presently.

Without having heard Orville, Landon confirmed the assertion. "They were an influential family back then." I tried not to let Orville's offended demeanor at the use of past tense distract me.

"I admit, I'm not very smart about legal stuff," I said,

frowning down at the parchment. "Can you tell me what all of this means?"

Landon nodded excitedly. "Of course!" His cheeks filled with color, and I suspected that he would do this work for free, were it not for his need to support a family now. "The penitentiary was constructed hundreds of years ago. It was called Eastwind Penitentiary for most of its history. Before the sale, it was much smaller, too. Fifty-five years ago"—he pointed to a paragraph at the start of the newspaper article—"the High Council decided that it wasn't in the town's budget to keep operating it on the taxes they collected. So they decided to sell it off to a private owner."

I scrunched up my nose. "Who would want to own a prison?"

"A lot of people, apparently."

"Why?"

"Whoever owns the prison likely has some power in the town, yeah? Like, you can let out whomever you want and make people you don't like disappear." He crinkled up his nose. "Icky, I know."

"Unfortunately," I said, "I'm starting to be cynical enough to understand what you're talking about. I don't relate to the desire for power, but if this case is teaching me anything, it's how much the promise of power and influence can blind people to more important things." I stared down at the paper. "You said the penitentiary had only been named after the Ironhelms for fifty-three years, but the High Council decided to sell it fifty-five years ago. What happened during those two years?"

His face lit up again at the question. "Great attention to detail, Dahlia! Yes, there are two years in there between the announcement of the sale and the closing of the sale. What happened was a bidding war. And, I would assume, quite a bit of bribery and shady dealings."

I shot Orville's ghost a sideways glance. "Sounds about right."

The spirit huffed and put his back to me.

"Who were the Ironhelms in a bidding war with?" I asked.

"The Hardhearts."

"The Hardhearts? Wait," I said. "That name. I've heard that name before. Are there Hardhearts in Eastwind?"

"A few, assuming they've survived this long in prison."

"What?!"

"If any of the Hardhearts are still in Eastwind, they're in the penitentiary. According to this article, the bidding war turned ugly. They resorted to criminal accusations. Apparently, the Ironhelms accused the Hardhearts of bribing all kinds of Eastwind officials. The Hardhearts went on trial for bribery, and the star witness who is credited with swaying the jury was..." He could hardly contain his excitement. "You won't believe this."

But I did believe it. I already knew, because I remembered where I'd heard that name before. "Orville Ironhelm."

"Yes!"

"The goblin who was just murdered in town this weekend."

"You keep talking about me like I'm not right here," snapped Orville. "It's downright disrespectful."

I turned toward the spirit and said, "If you would just answer my questions, I wouldn't have to go to all this trouble!"

"I've told you nothing but the truth," insisted Orville. "You simply don't want to believe me."

"Unicorn swirls!" I said, borrowing a local phrase. "That's a bunch of hot, steaming unicorn swirls, and you know it. Or... maybe you don't. But either way, you haven't helped me get to the bottom of *anything*, and here I am trying to help *you* in my free time!"

"Oh please," he spat. "Don't flatter yourself. You aren't trying to help me. You're trying to impress that bumbling deputy."

"Stu isn't bumbling," I replied. "He's just overworked. Something you wouldn't know anything about."

Orville crossed his arms. "It's true. I've worked as hard as any dignified artisan should. It's disgraceful to exert oneself to the point of exhaustion."

Boy, oh boy, I'd had just about enough of this goblin.

He was right on one thing: I wasn't doing any of this for him.

I could tell Landon was staring a hole through me as I argued with what appeared to him to be empty air, but I wasn't ready to let Orville off the hook yet. "Why did you testify against the Hardhearts?" I demanded.

"They were guilty of bribery, and I had proof."

"And *your* family?" I said. "Were they also guilty of bribery?"

He smirked. "We weren't the ones on trial."

"And what evidence was there against them?"

He shrugged. "How would I know? I'm not a detective. Unlike you, I don't even *pretend* to be one."

Landon leaned forward. "That's Orville, right? What's he saying?"

I glared at the ghost. "Do you know if there are any free Hardhearts in Eastwind?"

Orville rolled his eyes. "I don't even know if there are any imprisoned Hardhearts in Eastwind. For all I know, each of them died in that prison long ago."

"For bribery?" I asked. "Tell me they didn't get life in prison for *that*."

"No, no. They only got a few years each for the bribery charges."

"Then why would any of them still be in there?" I asked.

He shrugged as if this were starting to bore him. "For bad behavior."

"What?"

"I didn't keep up with it, but before I left Eastwind

for Avalon, I remember hearing that they were causing trouble in the penitentiary and kept getting additional time tacked on."

"*All* of them?" I asked incredulously.

"Yes, that's what I heard."

"You really want me to believe that every Hardheart in prison was causing enough trouble to get years tacked onto their sentence? In a penitentiary owned and run by the family who put them in prison after an ugly bidding war?"

He dismissed my incredulity with a flick of the wrist. "Believe what you want, but don't keep claiming I won't tell you anything useful. I'm telling you my truth. Your choice not to believe it is hardly my problem." He sighed. "This is droll and unflattering." Then he disappeared.

"*Feels like you might've been getting to close to the truth,*" said Atlas. "*I think he's allergic to it.*"

"*Unless the truth happens to make him look good,*" I replied. "*I doubt that happens often, but even a stopped clock is right twice a day.*"

"Is he still here?" asked Landon cautiously.

I turned toward him. "No. He left."

"Anything interesting?"

"Not really. He doesn't know of any Hardhearts who might still be in Eastwind, whether free or in the penitentiary."

"You think they wouldn't still be in the penitentiary for a bribery char..." He didn't need as much help as I did to arrive there. "Oh. Right. Probably some bribery involved on the part of the Ironhelms."

I looked down at the copy of the *Eastwind Watch* again. "There aren't any Ironhelms in Eastwind anymore, and there aren't any Hardhearts in Eastwind anymore, is that right?"

"None that I know of," said Landon, "but that doesn't..."

I didn't hear the rest of what he had to say, because my gaze landed on an image farther down the article that I hadn't noticed before. It was a small, hand-drawn illustration. Two crests that appeared to be colliding with one another.

I only recognized one of the crests, but I could deduce the rest. The one I didn't recognize had a hefty battle helmet with the visor drawn in the center of it. The one I *did* recognize, positioned in opposition to the first in the illustration, had a heart with a sword through it. I'd just seen that same crest on Lilac's locket.

"This says the Hardhearts' seventeen-year-old daughter managed to escape Eastwind before she could be imprisoned with the rest of her family." I pointed to the line in the article. "How old would she be today?"

Landon's blond brows rose up his forehead as he did the math. "Approximately seventy, depending on her birthday."

I tried to make it all fit together. "Maybe a grand-mother, then."

"Huh?"

"Landon, I've seen that crest before in this investigation. I think I know of a Hardheart in Eastwind."

"One that's not in the penitentiary?"

I nodded. "She's very much free." But maybe not for long.

Chapter Eighteen

After stopping by Time to Kiln, where Raven supplied me with exactly what I needed, Atlas and I headed straight to Cair Crestfall. I was worried I might be too late, so I stopped by the front desk as soon as we entered the lobby.

Ferin looked up and went wide-eyed, likely at the sight of a Fifth Wind and a hellhound rushing at him, then managed to muster up a customer service smile. "Dahlia. Can I help you?"

"Is Lilac still here or did she already leave?"

"I can't give informa—"

"Please! It's urgent."

"I didn't see her leave this morning."

"And did Malavic come by at all?"

"The Count?"

"Yes, the Count. The owner of this hotel who's

comping her room." I didn't add how I suspected he was involved in a murder, too. "Did he come by?"

"No. He hasn't been in. Do you need to speak with him?"

Oh, I'd be speaking with him, all right.

...Unless I could simply leave that to Sheriff Bloom.

"No, it's fine. Thank you." I nodded for Atlas to follow me, and we hurried up the staircase toward the guest rooms.

"Your heart is racing so loud I can hardly hear myself think," said Atlas as we arrived at Lilac's room.

I inhaled deeply. *"You're right."* I closed my eyes. If she was in there, this could wait another few seconds while I calmed myself. Focus was what I needed now. Focus and a little courage.

Or a *lot* of courage.

"Now it's just my heart that's racing," said Atlas. *"Do you think she's going to curse us?"*

"Oh. Um, I hadn't actually thought about that. I suppose she is a witch, right?"

"She may also try to bop us," he added. *"Right on the head."*

"I doubt that'll be her go-to," I replied. I loved my familiar, but he proved that anxiety could be contagious. I didn't need to think about everything that could go wrong here. *"Why don't you wait in the hallway? Keep watch, and bark if anyone arrives."*

"Like Malavic?"

"Especially Malavic."

"What about a minotaur on a rampage?"

"Good grief. Yes, bark about that, too. But... no more scenarios, please." I knocked on the door and quickly heard, "Who is it?" coming from inside the room.

"It's Dahlia Wildes," I said, trying not to imagine a rampaging minotaur entering this already dangerous situation. "I wanted to see how you're doing after our talk yesterday."

"I'm fine," she replied without opening the door. I pressed my ear to the wood and heard footsteps and indistinct clunking.

Okay. That approach didn't work. "I discovered some new information, and I'd like to share it with you. In private."

The sounds from the other side of the door stopped.

A few more footsteps, then the door swung open, and I was face to face with Lilac.

Orville Ironhelm's killer.

"Can I come in?" I looked past her, and sure enough, she was in the middle of packing.

Her gaze found Atlas in the hallway behind me. "I'm allergic."

"That's fine. He can stay out here."

Atlas made a show of sitting and staying.

She wasn't impressed. "You said you had new information. What is it?"

"I shouldn't be sharing it with anyone, but he was your boss, so I thought you deserved to know."

"Then tell me."

I looked up and down the hallway. No other guests were lingering, but hopefully the possibility of someone opening their door would be enough. "It's sensitive information. Deputy Manchester wouldn't like it if he knew I told you. Can I come in? Atlas will stay out here."

She pushed her glasses up her nose, sighed, then said, "Fine. Make it quick."

I walked past her into the room. She had a large suitcase open on the bed, half of the clothes folded neatly inside it, the other half wrinkled up and shoved in there haphazardly. She was in a hurry to leave. Perhaps I'd shown up just in time.

"Tell me what you need to tell me," she said. "I have a train to catch."

"You're not staying in Eastwind, then?"

"Of course not."

"But I thought you wanted to be somewhere people supported one another."

"It was a nice dream," she said, gathering up her cosmetics from the vanity and tossing them carelessly into a small pouch, "but I've managed to provide for myself on my own my whole life. I'd be kidding myself to think I could be part of a community now. I'm not made for it. I wish I were, but I'm not. Now tell me what you have to say. I don't want to miss my train."

On the walk over, I'd thought of a dozen different ways to ease into the topic I'd come here to discuss. Unfortunately, I'd forgotten all of them. "I know you killed Orville."

Lilac stopped packing, a scarf dangling in her hand as she spun to face me. "I didn't."

"You did. But I don't think it was on purpose, and that does matter here."

She blinked rapidly. "I didn't kill him. I'm not responsible for his death. You don't know what you're talking about." But there was fear in her eyes, and I felt a sharp emotion like a dagger thrust out at me, invisible but tangible all the same.

"I don't believe you meant for it to happen," I repeated. "I think that's why you were so scared when I first tried to speak with you."

She put her hands on her hips and glared at me. "You have *no* idea what you're talking about. You're insane, aren't you? I've heard that about Fifth Winds."

I tried to steady my breathing, but I was getting light-headed with fear—whether hers or mine, I wasn't sure. Probably both. Even though she appeared calm and confident, her stillness reminded me of a trapped animal. When the danger closed in, would the animal lash out? I'd soon find out.

"You're a Hardheart. That crest on your locket. It's the family crest. Am I right?"

She gripped her locket so tightly her knuckles turned white. "My last name isn't Hardheart."

"Because it was your grandmother's name, right? Your mother took some other name, didn't she?"

Her spring-loaded silence all but confirmed my suspicions.

"You knew Orville had something to do with your family's situation, which was presumably not a good one after your grandmother escaped to Avalon with nothing to her name. I believe those things you told me about your childhood, how hard it was. I believe you were telling me the truth, Lilac. I understand why you would hate the Ironhelms, if you suspected they were the reason you had to strike out on your own at twelve. They had most of your family locked away to secure ownership of the prison, took whatever wealth and assets the Hardhearts had, then, if what I suspect is true, made sure your family never got out. Orville's testimony was crucial to all of that happening, and I can understand why you would hate him for it.

"It was all suspicion and hearsay for most of your life, though, wasn't it? Then, at the competition, you finally got a partial confession. It was wrapped up in all the other bribery, but you heard him tell the truth, something that's admittedly a rarity for him. I don't think that confession was an accident, though. I think you orchestrated it. Not on your own, but with help from someone in town.

"But it wasn't enough for you. It was just a snippet, not the whole story. And you were owed the whole story after what you'd been through, weren't you? So when you returned to the hotel with him, you helped him into his room and offered to make him some tea, didn't you? You spiked his drink with the same powder you gave to Margot to create her glaze. The dragon scales."

Lilac looked like she was the one seeing a ghost, and she shook her head as if in a daze.

I kept pushing on. I was too deep now to back out. "You wanted a *full* confession. You wanted him to humiliate himself with the truth about what he did to your family, but also anything else he would cough up. But you pushed it too far. You didn't know that making someone who was so disconnected from the truth confess to all those things might push his body too far. You didn't know that it would stop his heart. Did I get that right?"

"No," she said, hardly above a whisper, but her eyes were filling with tears.

I wasn't enjoying any of this. Every word of my suspicions, every accusation, hurt to say. I saw so much of my own misfortune in her life that I could imagine myself standing where she was, a scarf gripped loosely in one hand, a locket of my distant family in the other, feeling my future slip away.

"You can't prove any of that," she said.

"I can." I reached into my pocket and pulled out the small velvet satchel with the evidence Raven had given me from the studio. Slowly, I extended the evidence toward her, offering it up.

She squinted down at the bag, and I understood why she would find it puzzling. She'd never seen the satchel before. "The evidence is inside of it," I muttered.

Cautiously, she set the scarf on the bed and took the velvet bag from me, weighing it in her hand, then loosening the drawstring and carefully emptying the contents into her palm.

At first, it was clear she didn't know what she was seeing. Then her eyes went wide.

"You're right," she said. "I killed him and it was an accident."

I was relieved to see that the truth glaze worked just as well when it was only on a shard of the original vase. Raven had since destroyed the rest of it for obvious reasons, but she'd snuck me a piece of it for this purpose.

Continuing to stare down at the object in her hand, Lilac continued her confession. "You don't know how long I've spent trying to understand why what happened to my family happened. I knew something had transpired, but it wasn't until I received an anonymous letter about the job opportunity with Orville that I started to put the pieces together."

"An anonymous tip?" I said.

"Yes, but in retrospect, I believe it was from Count Malavic. He's the one who gave me the powder to sneak into one of the contestants' glazes. When I saw how desperate Margot was to win on the first day of the competition, I knew I could entice her to do it."

"You approached her in a cloak," I said.

"I did. And she didn't ask any questions. She took the powder and used it, just as I'd hoped."

As Malavic had hoped, I thought but didn't say.

"Why did Malavic want you to get the powder into the glaze?" I asked.

"He wanted the confession from Orville as much as I did. He wants the penitentiary."

"Why?"

"I don't know, he didn't say."

I had no choice but to believe her on that, so I didn't press the question. Instead, I asked, "You've been working with Malavic this whole time?"

"He's been helping me. I've needed these answers for years. He's the only person who's offered to help me in my entire life. Of course I'm going to accept his help. Judge me if you want, but if *you're* honest with yourself, you can't say you wouldn't do the same."

"I certainly wouldn't take help from Malavic," I said.

"Liar. He's a generous man. Not perfect, but generous. The most generous stranger I've met."

I knew better than to argue with her on that. It might not be the objective truth, but it was *her* truth.

"And what did learning the truth from Orville do for you?" I asked. "Why did you need it from him?"

"What did it *do* for me?" She stared at me incredulously, like I'd just asked whether air was necessary. "The truth doesn't need to serve a purpose to deserve being heard. I deserved to hear the truth. And *he* deserved to have to say it."

"Even though it killed him?"

She scowled, her nostrils flaring with rage. "Even though it killed him."

Her knuckles were white from gripping the shard, and I wouldn't have been surprised if its sharp edges were drawing blood. The intensity from her seemed to fill the whole room. I tried to name the emotion and settled on righteousness. The energy felt white-hot, whatever it was.

"One last question," I said. "Why are you still holding that thing?" I nodded at her clenched fist. "You just confessed to me. You didn't have to. You could've let it go."

Her upper lip twitched, and then her snarl faded. Her shoulders relaxed, and she looked down at her closed fist. With what appeared to be great effort, she opened up her hand, revealing the glazed shard that sparkled in the lamplight of the room. "I didn't want to let it go," she said. "But now..." She let the piece fall to the floor. It clattered across the tiles and came to a rest hardly a foot away from me.

For a moment, neither of us spoke, only stared at the glimmering ceramic on the floor.

"You *wanted* me to know what you'd done?" I asked.

She sounded tired now. "Someone needed to know the full truth besides me."

"You're not worried about being arrested?"

"Not particularly." She looked up, meeting my eye. "Just because I've told you these things doesn't mean there's evidence of it. Go tell the sheriff what I've told you. Maybe she'll believe you, but she can't prove it. I didn't leave any evidence. If Orville's ghost is anything like the living version, he can't be believed, either. Plus, he doesn't know how he died. He didn't see me put anything in his drink... because I didn't." She smiled, enjoying her renewed ability to lie.

For a moment, I thought she had me. It was true that it would only be my word to go on. Margot couldn't identify who'd provided her the powdered dragon scales, and no one had seen Lilac put anything into Orville's tea, not even Orville himself. It made perfect sense for her to be in his room with him after helping him back from the competition, since she was his assistant. She hadn't killed him with a spell that could be traced back to her wand, and she had a perfectly reasonable explanation for why any of her fingerprints might be in his room, on his doorknob, or on the teacup (assuming fingerprinting was a thing in Eastwind, which I wasn't entirely sure about; forensic science wasn't a huge thing here because magic could usually be relied on instead).

What evidence was there to prove to Sheriff Bloom that what I relayed to her about Lilac's confession was the truth?

Ah, but it was so obvious.

The truth.

I reached down and grabbed the vase shard from the ground. I'd avoided making skin contact with it up until that point, so I hadn't expected the crisp clarity that ran through my body like icy spring water.

It wasn't that I couldn't think of a lie, it was that the idea of speaking one seemed impossible and completely nonsensical. There was no appeal to it. Meanwhile, the clarity of truth felt obvious, like a pathway I'd been born to walk. I felt no fear of the truth. It was my friend, my guide, my protector. I ran toward it.

"I'm absolutely in love with Dante," I said.

Lilac scrunched up her nose. "Huh?"

"Shoot!"

"Who?"

I threw the clay piece into my pocket to stop touching it. "Forget I said that." I blinked back the afterglow of the glaze to refocus. "I don't need evidence to convince Sheriff Bloom. She has the gift of Judgment, and I'll simply tell her the truth." I nodded to the piece of broken pottery in my pocket. "She'll believe me."

Lilac's blue eyes grew large behind her thick lenses as it dawned on her what I meant to do.

If the glaze could be proven to have powdered dragon scales in it, which would be easy enough to test, then all I had to do was touch it when I spoke with the sheriff. I'd be compelled to tell the truth, and I could repeat Lilac's confession with complete honesty. Sheriff Bloom's angelic power of Judgment meant she could tell when someone was lying. As long as I stuck to the truth, which I would have to, it might be enough...

"You... you're going to get me arrested? In Eastwind?" Lilac's chest heaved as she appeared to stare right through me. "I'm gonna end up in *Ironhelm Penitentiary?*"

Oh no. Fangs and claws. I hadn't thought that far through this whole thing.

The idea of her ending up there horrified me. Terror

pulsed off her, but more importantly, I understood that *that* prison for her, a descendant of the Hardhearts who'd just killed an Ironhelm, wouldn't be like prison for the average criminal.

She hadn't meant to kill him, but she had. Maybe she would get a lesser charge. Then again, her relatives had only gone in for bribery, and as far as anyone knew, they'd never made it back out again. Any sentence for a Hardheart was, it seemed, a death sentence.

"Lilac, I have to tell Sheriff Bloom. I can't just let you go."

"I'm not going to the penitentiary!" Eyes wild, she drew her wand and pointed it directly at me. She'd be leaving all kinds of evidence if she killed me with a spell now, but she might make it back to Avalon before anyone knew it was her. Once she was there, she could disappear or travel to one of the other realms connected to that one. She could get away forever.

And I would be dead.

Maybe for good this time.

I held up my hands, wishing more than ever that I was the useful kind of witch who could wield a wand. "Please don't," was all I could think of to say.

"I didn't mean to kill him. You know that. I don't deserve to be locked away. I was trying to get to the truth! That's what *you're* doing here, too, isn't it? Trying to get to the truth. Do you deserve to be in Ironhelm for it? Never seeing the light of day again?" Fear was beginning to slur her words, and I worried what that might mean for my survival as her wand remained aimed at my chest.

Maybe I could let her go. Let her get away. Give her a second chance at life, now that she had the answers she'd been searching for. Perhaps she wasn't a danger to anyone else.

The memory of the clarity I'd felt when touching the glaze returned to me.

No, the truth's only job was to exist. If I could have mercy for her in my heart, understanding the full story, perhaps the sheriff could as well.

That was, if I lived long enough to speak with Gabby Bloom.

Summoning the truth to me, I said, "I don't want you to go to Ironhelm, Lilac."

"But I will if you tell the sheriff."

"We don't know that."

She shook her wand as she demanded, "Are you going to tell her?"

I cringed, braced for pain. Did she want the truth? Did she expect me to give that when my life was on the line?

I saw a decision flicker behind her eyes, but I wasn't sure where she would land.

Then suddenly she tossed her wand into her open suitcase, slammed the whole thing shut, and charged at me with it in her arms.

I was so shocked by the fact that she hadn't cursed me that my feet were seemingly stuck to the floor. Not a problem for her. She plowed right into me, using her suit-case as a battering ram, and knocked me right out of her path to escape.

My back hit the doorframe awkwardly, knocking the wind out of me. I tried to holler to Atlas that she was making a break for it, but I couldn't get enough air in my lungs.

Oh, right. Telepathy.

"Atlas! Don't let her escape!"

I heard a crash and a thud in the hallway and hoped to all things good that it wasn't the sound of Atlas turning tail and running, freaked out by a witch and her heavy luggage charging right at him.

When I was finally able to clamber to my feet, I found Lilac pinned to the floor in the hallway beneath the large white hellhound. I couldn't tell who was trem-bling harder. "Stay where you are, Lilac, and he won't bite."

"Bite? And expose my head to a bopping? Not a chance," he said.

"She doesn't need to know that."

When a tall elf stuck her head out of her room to observe the ruckus, likely to judge it more than do anything about it, I hollered for her to send for the deputy. She nodded and disappeared into her room again.

"Don't send me to Ironhelm!" Lilac whimpered. "I'll die there. You know I'll die there. I didn't mean for any of this to happen. I'm... I'm innocent!"

"I wouldn't go that far," I said. I leaned over her luggage to dig through it for her wand. Poor Stu didn't need that kind of a greeting.

I knew the second I leaned over the suitcase that I'd made a mistake. I felt the weight of the object in my pocket shift, and the shard came tumbling out, landing in Atlas's thick fur.

He shivered. *"It was me! I ate the plate of food off the counter at Medium Rare the other day! It was delicious and I don't regret a thing!"*

Chapter Nineteen

"You'd better leave that with me," Sheriff Bloom said as I stood to leave her cluttered office.

I stared down at the piece of clay, its dangerous glaze glittering under the harsh lights of the sheriff's office.

"Evidence," she gently reminded me.

I set it on one of the teetering stacks of paper on her desk.

"You believe everything I told you?" I said, once she tucked it away into a drawer.

"I do."

"Enough to charge her?"

"Assuming the test of this evidence comes back positive for dragon scales, yes."

"And then what?"

We'd already discussed the "and then what" at the very start of the conversation. It'd been the pretext for my telling her everything I knew. Only when I was sure she understood *why* I'd made the request prior to working with her was I satisfied enough to begin explaining why Stu had Orville's young assistant in handcuffs in one of the holding cells.

"And then," she began, "I'll make sure she's not tried in Eastwind. I'll put my force behind making sure she never enters Ironhelm."

"But she *is* going to serve some time, isn't she?" I asked, hating the idea of it.

I know it sounds crazy, but I didn't believe she was a bad person with bad intentions. Lilac was merely a lost person who fell in with the wrong crowd—namely, Count Malavic. The more I learned about him, the more I felt confident that Nora had been right about him all this time. She was usually right about people.

"I'm only the sheriff," said Bloom. "I don't know how the trial will play out. They do things a little different in Avalon. But she'll have a lawyer, and maybe it'll even be one who knows what they're doing. Since this was an accidental death, if she serves time, my hope is that it won't be long."

"She's not a danger to the public," I said.

Bloom rolled her shoulders back, her large white wings adjusting as she did. "Maybe not. You never know, though, Dahlia. You just never know." She motioned toward the door, and I knew she had other things to move on to. "I'll speak with the High Council. Call in some favors to get her transferred back to Avalon."

"Call in some favors with Malavic, you mean?" I

didn't know where my brazenness came from. Perhaps the glaze had a stronger afterglow than I realized.

But Sheriff Bloom just laughed. "Oh, he certainly owes me a *lot* of favors, and not just for this. I let his nonsense go uncontested far too often sheerly due to my own busyness."

"Will he be arrested as well?"

Bloom suddenly looked as tired as I knew she felt. "No. He'll be fined for the dragon scales, but not much. He has a dragon, so fining him for possession won't stick. And he didn't sell them to Lilac, he simply gave her the powder, so there's no sale to fine him for. I'll dig around in the code and see if there's something about intent to distribute that I can slap him with for grinding up the scales into powder, but that's probably the best I can do."

"That hardly feels like justice."

"You don't have to tell *me* that." She paused. "I'll do right by Lilac as much as I can, Dahlia. I promise. I don't want to send her to Ironhelm Penitentiary any more than you want to see her there. Now that I know who she is and what might happen to her behind those walls, *that* wouldn't be justice either. She did still cause a goblin's death, though."

"I understand." Not wanting to take up any more of the generous sheriff's time, I left the office.

Atlas was sitting with his backside pressed into a corner in the lobby of the sheriff's department when I appeared. As I approached, ready to stick a fork in this investigation and go back to my everyday life, Stu poked his head out of his office. "Miss Wildes." He strolled over. "Good work. I can't thank you enough for helping out on this." He held out a small leather pouch, and I looked down at it, unsure what I was supposed to do. "From discretionary spending," he said.

"Stu, you don't have to—"

"Maybe I just *want* to," he said, cutting me off uncharacteristically. "I can't promise that it'll be a regular thing—that depends on the budget from the High Council—but I was sinking into the swamp this time, and you pulled me out. We have the killer in a jail cell, and I can wrap up some of my reports from the other calls this weekend. Take it."

I took the bag. It was heavier than I expected. I peeked inside. Gold and silver gleamed back at me. "Sweet baby Jackalope, Stu. What am I gonna do with all this?"

"Make dinner plans with Mr. Fontaine? Somewhere nice." He winked.

My heart fluttered in my chest, but I couldn't tell if it was more out of nervousness or excitement. "That sounds like a great idea."

"What sounds like a great idea?" came another voice from the entrance of the building.

I turned and saw Tanner strolling in, out of uniform.

"You're back," said Stu, sounding like he might cry or jump up and do a heel click. Maybe both.

"Yeah, we're back," said Tanner.

I asked, "How was it?"

"It was... interesting. Good."

"Relaxing?" asked Stu.

Tanner hedged slightly. "Almost. As relaxing as a place designed for were-beast comfort can be to a couple of witches. Ansel and Jane had a great time." He paused and narrowed his eyes at me, the significance of my presence in this building sinking in. "What happened?"

Stu shook his head and clapped Tanner on the shoulder. "Don't worry about it. Miss Wildes and I have it handled."

Chapter Twenty

Dante was fresh off a long shift at Franco's Pizza and wasn't up for a fancy dinner that night, which was fine with me. We could always do one of those later.

And I knew there would be a later with us. There had to be. I would make sure of it.

So instead of something high end, we made plans to meet at Medium Rare for greasy burgers and some chips and queso. That was just fine by me.

When I walked in, the dining room was crowded with dinner guests. Atlas and I paused as we stepped inside. *"Are you mad at me?"* he said.

"Huh?"

"About eating that plate of food off the counter."

Oh right. His confession. *"No. And if you promise not to do it again, I won't tell Nora about it."* He agreed to those terms and wove his way through the tables toward his usual spot behind the counter, where servers made a habit of tossing scraps to whatever hellhounds happened to be posted up there.

That left me standing by myself. I looked around for Dante, but it seemed like he hadn't arrived yet. Not a big surprise. He'd wanted to go home and change after being cut from his shift so he didn't show up still smelling like pasta sauce. While I loved the smell of pasta sauce myself, I understood that being covered in a single smell all day, no matter how nice it was, started to wear on your morale. I used to spend all day smelling like cleaning solution, and while it was nice to know I was clean... yeah, it got old.

Ted was seated in his usual corner booth and waved at me as I caught sight of him. Perfect. I'd been meaning to catch up.

He set down his crossword puzzle as I approached. "Good to see you, Dahlia!"

"Good to see you, Ted. You happen to run into Orville this evening?"

He nodded. "I did. And I told him everything you told me to tell him."

"And?"

"He didn't believe it. Refused to accept that the truth had killed him."

"Sounds like something someone like him would refuse to believe," I said. "I guess he's still hanging around, then?"

"Nope."

I jerked my head back. "Oh?"

"Not to brag, but I'm good at what I do. Heh. After ushering thousands of spirits, I've learned that not everyone who really needs to get moving on is or ever will be ready to go. Doesn't change that it's definitely time for them to head out."

"And Orville? He needed to head out?"

"Did you meet the guy? What would he do lingering around here? Not like he'd keep himself busy in the library."

Fair point.

"I never force them to go," said Ted, "but I do my best to convince them."

"How'd you convince someone like Orville? He was so set on recovering his reputation here before he moved on."

"I told him that, on the other side, everyone already knows the truth about his reputation."

"And that was appealing to him?"

"It was. Some folks, like Orville, think they have the truth of the matter all the time. It's everyone *else* who's wrong. He wanted everyone to agree with him more than anything else in this realm. So, I told him that's what would happen when he passed over."

"Is that true?"

Ted shrugged. "Pretty sure. I didn't tell him he'd probably be the one to change his views on things, but either way, there's no hiding from the truth once you pass over."

"Bravo," I said, clapping politely. "I didn't think it could be done."

"Heh. What can I say? Reaping souls has taught me a thing or two about people."

"I'll have to tap you for your wisdom sometime," I said. "I still feel like I know nothing about people. I don't even know all that much about myself."

"Happy to help. Later." He nodded his hooded head toward the door. "Your date just arrived."

My heart leaped up into my throat as I spotted Dante scanning the diner. When he caught sight of me, I waved.

Now was the time to be honest, even if it killed me.

We grabbed an empty booth by the front windows, and before sliding in across from each other, I grabbed him on the arm and leaned in. His expression softened into a smile, and he moved in and kissed me. Nothing too salacious in public—that wasn't either of our style—but it was still nice. I could tell it meant a lot to him, too.

He was nervous. It wasn't hard to guess why, considering my behavior since he first touched Margot's vase and said he was in love with me.

We sat across from each other, and I opened my mouth to dive right in before my nerves could get the best of me. Didn't happen. At that exact moment, someone appeared at the table with a coffee pot and two mugs in her hand. "I already got Atlas some scrambled eggs," said Nora, pouring our coffee.

"How was Wisconsin?" Dante asked.

Nora sighed. "I don't think I'm built for vacation. It feels good to be home, where everything is familiar, I know what I'm supposed to be doing, and the days run pleasantly together. I didn't miss anything while I was gone, did I?"

Dante and I shared a quick glance. "Not too much," I said. "I'll catch you up at home."

She looked from Dante to me, and it seemed to click for her that something unspoken was lingering in the air. She cleared her throat. "What can I get y'all to eat?"

We put in our order, and once she scurried away, I started in before I could chicken out again.

"I wasn't being honest," I said.

His brows pinching together, he pointed after Nora. "When you ordered?"

"No."

"Then when do you mean?"

"That's hard to say. For a while, I guess. Definitely when we had dinner last night."

"Okay…" I could tell it was taking a lot from him to remain calm. "Go on."

I braced myself and looked him in the eyes, like he deserved. "I love you."

A smile bloomed on his face, but he reined it in quickly. "Are you sure?"

"What?" I hadn't expected *that* response. "Of course I'm sure!"

"How much do you love me?"

I blinked. "How much do I—"

He laughed and quickly grabbed my hands on the tabletop. "I love you too. And you didn't have to say it to me, Dahlia. I know the words make you uncomfortable. It made me feel the same way, which is why you only heard it from me when I touched the vase."

"You're not mad it took me this long to say it?"

"How could I be mad when I was nervous about it, too? And when you've shown me that you love me through your actions? That's not a thing to get mad about."

He scooted around to sit next to me in the booth and put his arm around my shoulder, pulling me close to his firm side. I inhaled the faint and pleasant smell of him, a mixture of pine and moss that seemed baked into his skin from his childhood on Fluke Mountain. I indulged in the warmth of this man next to me who made the effort to understand me and who saw me deeply and gave me the benefit of the doubt.

I'd been scared of the truth that my heart had known for quite some time. Scared that in speaking the truth, it would trap me and commit me to something I didn't want.

Instead, the truth did what it does best: it set my heart free.

Dante leaned over and kissed me on the top of my head, keeping his arm firmly around me as I closed my eyes and enjoyed the warmth of his breath in my hair.

The truth didn't have to serve a purpose to matter, but in this case, speaking it aloud made all the difference.

Epilogue

I couldn't believe how quickly Dante had managed to organize this event. For the second Friday in a row, a crowd of locals and tourists alike had gathered outside of Time to Kiln, as many of them had done just the week before for the competition.

Dante and I stood at the back of the crowd, partially so he could survey the entire scene, but also because it was the most comfortable place for me. Atlas had agreed to do himself a favor and stay home, so long as I promised to stay close to Dante in case I became overwhelmed with emotions again and needed someone to steady me and pull me to safety.

Dante had an arm around my shoulder, and I kept one around his waist, enjoying the steadiness of his body. I was so proud of what he'd pulled together, and even more proud of how the town had joined up so quickly to make it happen.

Liberty Freeman had volunteered his time to play auctioneer, and he did it so well that I had to assume he'd done it many times before.

On either side of the crowd were long tables of refreshments to keep everyone comfortable. Argienta, who owned Hagseed Café, had donated platters of small sandwiches. Fiona Sheehan had closed the pub for the afternoon to set up a pop-up bar where she served cold brews from the keg and made sure everyone stayed hydrated. Ezra Ares had offered the same tents that he'd rented out to Raven and Jude for the competition, but this time they were free of charge to ensure the crowd didn't get too hot to stick around. Darius Pine had even pulled some strings so that all the highest bidders would have a free steak dinner thrown in at Stews and Brews up on Fluke Mountain.

And, of course, the greatest generosity was from all of the pottery competition contestants, who banded together, at Dante's request, to offer up their entries along with the other finished pieces that hadn't made the cut for the final judging. All of the pottery was to be auctioned off, with all the proceeds going directly to Jude and Raven.

My only responsibility in this process had been helping Dante convince the studio owners to go public about the fact that they'd taken a loan, and if they couldn't repay it, the studio would end up under new ownership (we decided not to specify whose ownership that would be). I could tell they were still embarrassed to have entered into that agreement with the Count, but they saw sense eventually, and that allowed for Dante to put this whole amazing event together.

As Liberty held up the next item, a large platter with hand-painted roses beneath a transparent pearlescent glaze, and described it in such an enticing way that I almost felt compelled to bid on it myself, Grace wandered up to us at the back of the crowd. She had a small bowl of queso in one hand and was balancing a plate of tortilla chips on the crook of her elbow. "If you hold the plate, I'll let you have some."

I quickly grabbed the teetering plate; the food was a donation from Medium Rare, and I knew better than to turn down their creamy queso. Apparently, it'd won the town's cook-off back when Nora and Tanner first launched it, and I could understand why. Corn chips and melted cheese had a magic all their own. Culinary magic. I knew Nora would never tamper with the diner's food by adding spells to it, but it did sort of feel like I was struck by a serenity spell every time I had her chips and queso.

Today was no different. As soon as the melty cheese hit my tongue, I moaned. Dante didn't think twice to scoop himself some, too.

"I didn't think hot queso would go well with a sunny day," said Grace, "but I was wrong."

I pointed down at the food, and with my mouth still full, said, "This and a margarita, and I could die happy."

"A what?" said Grace.

At first, I thought she simply couldn't understand me because I'd garbled my words, but when I repeated myself and she still looked confused, I gasped. "You don't know what a margarita is?"

Grace shook her head.

I turned to Dante. It was clear he didn't know either.

"But how...?" It was true, I hadn't seen a single one since being here. But Nora had been here for years—she'd even brought chips and queso to the town. It felt like she'd fallen down on the job by not also bringing margaritas from our old realm to this one. "I'll speak to Nora and Fiona. Maybe even Jane," I said. "We'll get this sorted out."

Landon appeared from the same direction that Grace had a moment before. "What amount are we up to?" he asked Dante.

"Three pieces left to bid on, about nineteen golds short of the total Raven and Jude need."

Landon sucked in air. "You think it could still happen?"

Dante shrugged, but I could tell a dark mood was starting to settle in on him. The hope and anticipation that he'd carried with him earlier had thinned significantly as the bidding went on.

"Don't give up on it yet," I said quietly to him. "You never know who might come through."

The bidding on the hand-painted platter continued, and it was finally sold to Echo Chambers, one of the town's up-and-coming businesspeople. The faun appeared to enjoy the applause his winning bid earned him, and he waved to the crowd around him.

"That's gonna look great in one of your many fine establishments, Echo," said Liberty. "Everybody, be sure to drop by Lyre's Lounge and Echo's Salon while you're in town. Enjoy the fruits of Echo's labors." Liberty grinned and winked at the faun, who pressed his palms together and offered the genie a grateful bow back.

"Was that more or less than you expected it to go for?" asked Landon.

Dante shook his head vaguely. "I'm not a numbers guy. I didn't dig in that much to the calculations. Just figured if I could organize something, maybe the town would come together."

As luck would have it, the final piece for auction was Dante's teapot, the one that reminded me of a sunset. Raven and Malavic had been impressed with it during the competition. Orville less so.

But Orville was a fraud and is dead, so who cares what he thought?

I surprised myself with my own pettiness, but decided it was true enough to let it go.

Dante watched stoically as Liberty announced the teapot and ran through all its most desirable qualities, really selling the thing like I didn't think anyone else could've.

"It's not gonna pull in enough," Dante muttered.

"You don't know that," I said gently.

"We're still ten gold and five silvers short," he said.

I was still getting used to the strange currency in Eastwind—I hadn't been good with money in New Orleans, and I'd spent the first twenty-nine years of my life around the dollar—but I did know that ten gold and five silvers was a *lot* to expect for a single teapot. None of the pieces had fetched even half that price.

I certainly didn't have it on me, but I did have *some* gold on me, thanks to that stipend from the sheriff's department. I'd planned on using it to take Dante to a nice dinner, but I could tell this meant more to him. Much, much more. I wouldn't be able to nudge us over the finish line with what I had to my name, but maybe I could drive the price up so that someone else did.

Liberty announced the starting bid, and I immediately shot my hand into the air.

Dante snapped his head toward me. "What are you doing?"

"Bidding," I said innocently.

Grace chuckled.

"You don't have to do this, Dahl," he said.

Another hand shot into the air from the middle of the crowd.

"A gold and two coppers from Darius Pine," announced Liberty gleefully. "Can I get a gold and five coppers?"

I raised my hand, and Liberty announced it.

"There's no way you're going to outbid Darius," Dante muttered.

"I don't need to outbid him. I just need to make him bid higher."

Dante's mouth dropped open, then he laughed.

Darius Pine was best friends with Dante's uncle Ansel, making the leader of the werebears essentially family to Dante. The two of them often shifted forms and charged around the woods of Fluke Mountain together. While Darius was older than Dante by a solid decade and a half, the two of them had a competitive brotherly relationship.

Dante would definitely get a kick out of bleeding some money from the other werebear.

For a good cause, of course.

The bidding continued between us, and when we reached five golds, I knew I was way out of my depth. Darius still seemed in it to win it, though, so despite not having the money to back up my bid, I stuck my hand up one more time. Before Darius could top my bid, another hand shot up.

"Six golds."

The crowd gasped at the new voice entering into the war, but Ansel Fontaine kept his hand in the air, grinning at Darius over the heads of the crowd.

"Come on, man!" shouted Darius playfully. "You're really gonna do this to me? Six golds and a silver!"

Liberty called it out, and Ansel countered. The price rose to just over seven golds. We needed ten golds and five silvers to meet the amount Jude and Raven required to pay back the loan to Malavic and reclaim their studio as theirs.

It had clearly stopped being about Dante's teapot, as I suspected neither of these men drank tea. It was a great piece of artistry, sure, but no one in their right mind would pay this much for it off the shelf in the store. This was about pride now.

The bidding slowed to a grinding halt at seven golds, two silvers, and ten coppers. Liberty called it out, inquiring for any higher bids.

Going once...

Going twice...

It wasn't enough yet, and I felt a knot form in my stomach at the idea of getting so close but falling short. Maybe there was still something that could be done.

"Twelve gold, five silver and, uh, ten copper. Heh."

All eyes turned toward the source of the extraordinary bid.

Ted stood a few yards behind us, one hand gripping the scythe, the other holding a pile of coins in his gloved palm. "Would that be enough?" he asked me.

I couldn't speak.

"Yeah," said Dante slowly, "that would do it."

Ted held up the coins. "You got that, Liberty?"

Even the genie seemed stunned by the development. "Yes. Okay. Right. Twelve gold, five silver, and ten copper from Eastwind's very own reaper, Ted. Can I get twelve gold and six silver? Twelve gold, six— Aw, forget it. Once, twice, *sold* to Ted!"

The crowd went wild, and as Liberty wrapped up the event, Ted approached us. "It's a wonderful teapot, Dante. Reminds me of gazing out over the Murder-swamp on a beautiful Hallow's Eve."

Dante let out a big exhale, seemingly at a loss for words. Then he held out his hand. Ted dipped his head to stare at it, as if unsure what he was being asked to do. Then he dropped the coins into his pocket and shook the werebear's hand.

Dante was good about muffling the shudder that ran down his back as he made contact with Ted.

"I didn't know you had that kind of money," said Grace.

"You exist long enough and you end up with a little stockpile," said Ted. "Plus, I own my cabin in the Dead-woods outright, and no one has ever asked me to pay taxes on it. Heh. It also helps that I don't have to eat or drink if I don't feel like it. Makes living cheap."

"How do you earn money?" asked Grace.

Landon nudged her gently to signal she might be asking too blunt of a question, but she ignored him, and Ted didn't seem bothered.

"I work for the sheriff's department. I collect the bodies. You didn't think they asked me to do that for free, did you?"

"Yes," she said. "I did."

"To be fair," said Dante, "so did I."

"Me too," I admitted.

Ted laughed. "Well, obviously I *would* do it for free

if they needed me to, but no, Sheriff Bloom made sure I started getting paid fairly decades ago. Plus backpay for the years I did it for free. Ooh! I'd better collect my new teapot!"

The reaper made to leave, but Dante stopped him. "Wait. Thank you. Seriously, thank you. You didn't have to do it, but you did."

"You're welcome. But of course I had to do it if I could. That's what we do in Eastwind, right? We come together for each other."

"At least come by Franco's Pizza and let me buy your meals for a while."

Ted nodded. "I could do that. But I'd also like if the four of you—and Monte and Atlas, of course—come have tea with me at my cabin sometime."

"Deal," said Dante.

"Monte would love that," said Grace.

"And so would we," Landon added politely.

It would be a hard sell to get Atlas back into the Deadwoods, but I said, "I'd love to. Thanks for the invitation, Ted. We'll pick a day soon."

The reaper shot us a thumbs-up then glided toward the front of the crowd to collect his prized item.

Now that the main event was over, the packed crowd in front of us spread out toward the tables to enjoy all that was left of the donated food and drink.

Dante excused himself to go recap the excitement with Ansel and Darius, who I saw laughing and jawing with Liberty, and Grace and Landon hurried off to get a pint before the keg ran out, since they had a babysitter for the afternoon and might as well take advantage of it.

I spotted the witch Oliver Bridgewater unloading another keg for Fiona and couldn't help but laugh. This afternoon was promising to carry into a festive evening.

I wasn't alone for long before I felt someone standing right behind me. I sensed a void of emotions and could guess who it was before I even turned to look at him. "Count Malavic."

The vampire cradled a stemmed glass of red wine loosely in his palm and looked as displeased as I'd ever seen him. I couldn't imagine wanting to drink red wine outside on a hot day like this, but then again, I wasn't undead. Maybe Malavic didn't register the heat the way the living did. The phrase "cold, dead heart" came to mind, but I pushed it aside.

"Cute little event your boyfriend put together," he said, waving a hand at the studio like he was telling it to scram.

I felt such distaste for him, knowing what I did about how he'd manipulated the situation with Lilac. She would be the one charged with the crime, but she had no idea the potency of the powdered dragon scales she was giving Orville or what could happen when someone as estranged from reality as he was ingested the substance.

While I was happy she finally got answers to what had happened to her family that caused her to live in poverty and fend for herself from a young age, there had to be a way Malavic could've provided her with those answers without sneakily pulling strings behind the scenes so that she got the job as Orville's assistant and eventually murdered him.

But that would've been too close to philanthropy for Malavic's taste. No, he had to get something out of it for it to be worth the effort, and he had. The last of the Ironhelms was out of the picture. I wouldn't be surprised if the penitentiary had a new name soon. And as a little bonus, everyone now knew that Orville had been a fraud and a criminal, not the master potter of quality taste that everyone had once believed. Destroying the goblin's reputation was the cherry on top for Malavic, I bet.

I felt all that distaste building in my chest as I said, "Sorry your scheme to own the studio didn't work. You must be devastated."

"Ah, I never expected to own Time to Kiln," he said. "I was merely curious to see how it might play out if Raven and Jude couldn't pay me back on their own. Now I see."

"This was all... some sort of an experiment?" I said, hardly believing that anyone would treat someone's livelihood with such detached interest.

He swirled his wine. "Of a sort. Eastwind has changed a lot in the last few years, and it continues to change with each passing month. As a business owner, I must keep my finger on the pulse."

"You jealous this town still has a pulse?"

He arched his brows at me. "Feisty. I suspected you had a little of that in you."

"The whole town does. You think you can buy this place up, and put yourself in charge of everything, but you seemed to have forgotten that people show up for each other in Eastwind."

Malavic shrugged. "For now. That can change quickly, and when it does, I'll be ready. Oh, lighten up, my little death witch. It's a beautiful day. The town has come together. People are celebrating!"

"No thanks to you," I said.

"*All* thanks to me." He grinned. "A group that isn't tested from time to time falls apart, loses its sense of purpose, forgets its values. Were it not for me, this feeling you're surrounded by, this camaraderie, wouldn't exist in this moment. You're welcome."

"You should be on trial," I said. "You're just as responsible for Orville's death as Lilac was, if not more."

"How was I supposed to know a compulsive liar would have such a poor reaction to the truth?" But he smirked smugly as he said it. "I do believe I'll be seeing the inside of the prison soon, but not as punishment." He tapped a long, pale finger to his lips. "I think I'll keep the name, though. Malavic Manor Inn has a nice ring to it, but I don't think it would help my brand to have the penitentiary take my name. Yes, I think I'll keep it Iron-helm, in honor of its former owners. Far be it from me to deprive this town of its history."

Before I could respond, Ted appeared, holding up the teapot. "It's even prettier in person!"

Malavic conceded with a nod.

As Ted tucked it under his arm, he asked his long-time friend, "Are you mad at me?"

"No, Ted, I would expect nothing less from you."

"Oh good. Heh. You know I had to do it, right?"

Malavic nodded.

"It wasn't just for the studio and the people who enjoy it," Ted explained. "I also did it for you."

Malavic tilted his head back, squinting at the reaper. "Explain."

"We take care of each other in Eastwind," said Ted. "And sometimes that means keeping your friends from being a little evil."

Malavic laughed, finished the last of his wine, and clapped the reaper on the shoulder. "How about some scufflepuck once the pub opens back up tonight?"

"Darkness, yes!" Ted threw his robed arm around the vampire's shoulder, and the two of them walked off down the road, chatting scufflepuck strategy.

Eastwind had come together in ways I hadn't expected. And maybe Ted was right. It couldn't just be the people who liked one another that showed up for each other. It had to be *all* of us showing up for each other.

Even the imperfect Eastwinders. Even the ones who were, well, a little evil. ☾

About the Author

Nova Nelson grew up on a steady diet of Agatha Christie novels. She loves the mind candy of cozy mysteries and has been weaving paranormal tales since she first learned handwriting. Those two loves meet in her Eastwind Witches series, and it's about time, if she does say so herself.

When she's not busy writing, she enjoys pottery, talking to plants and eating breakfast for dinner.

Say hello:
nova@novanelson.com

facebook.com/thecozycoven

instagram.com/authornovanelson

bookbub.com/authors/nova-nelson

goodreads.com/nova_nelson

amazon.com/author/novanelson

More books from Eastwind

The Eastwind Witches Cozy Mysteries

Crossing Over Easy (Book 1)

Death Metal (Book 2)

Third Knock the Charm (Book 3)

Queso de los Muertos (Book 4)

Psych-Out (Book 5)

Gone Witch (Book 6)

Love Spells Trouble (Book 7)

Storm A-Brewin' (Book 8)

Hallow's Faire in Love and War (Book 9)

Dead Witch Walking (Book 10)

Old Haunts (Book 11)

First-Realm Problems (Book 12)

Happily Hereafter (Book 13)

The Ruby True Magical Mysteries

Werebear Scare (Book 1)

Elves' Bells (Book 2)

Vampire's Ire (Book 3)

The Dahlia Wildes Magical Mysteries

Find them here: www.eastwindwitches.com